To Vicky and Elise, with love, always…

The Undead Ravens

A Ludo Carstairs Supernatural Thriller

F.R. Jameson

LUDO CARSTAIRS SUPERNATURAL THRILLERS

The Nemesis Touch
The Mirror Demon
The Ghost Machine
The Crimson Snake
The Undead Ravens
The Wraith Assassin

PROLOGUE

Poor Garris suffered a lot of nightmares these days. Ludo didn't pry too much, but as far as he could understand, they related a great deal to wolves. Given his experiences (particularly what happened in Scotland eighteen months ago, and more recently, when they found themselves on the private island of an insane tech billionaire), this was perfectly understandable. And it was utterly commendable that he was seeking help to deal with these issues. To that end, when the two of them weren't immersed in a case, and Garris was in London, he went to therapy twice a week. And knowing this was one of those days was why Ludo Carstairs didn't tell his colleague about his little day trip to the English village of Little Buxberry. The place where, allegedly, the infamous horror author Jacob Ravens had been interred.

Actually, if Garris hadn't been otherwise engaged, there was a good chance Ludo wouldn't have mentioned this excursion to his friend anyway. It was a facet of himself he wasn't proud of, but which also gave him a secret joy in his heart. He liked to do his homework in private. It was, he felt, the magician in him. To him, it was always better to have the big reveal. He had been the same in school (or those periods of time when he'd focused his youthful attentions on school). He'd liked to astound his classmates by making pertinent and praiseworthy points pertaining to the novel which he had supposedly only flicked through. He'd enjoyed presenting his maths homework, showing no workings. When in fact, he'd been under the covers of his bed in the dorm, studying all night long. Absolutely, he knew it annoyed Garris when he would retrieve a beautifully formed gem which was perfect for the occasion, but he knew it thrilled his friend as well.

Hence, the trip to Little Buxberry. Ludo didn't know if coming here would give him anything, but he had to experience it for himself. He wanted to get a sense of the place. To see the sleepy churchyard where *something* had been buried. Maybe there would be nothing gained from his three and a half hour train commute (with half an hour waiting bored at Bristol Temple Meads Station, for a connection), but that wasn't important. If it was possible, to glean anything pertinent, then he'd bring it forth at the most opportune moment and Garris would be astonished.

Not long ago, Ludo and Garris had met a man named Elspeth Carmine. Elspeth was unusual, as he was more than one hundred and thirty years old, but resembled a man in his thirties. He was immortal and proud of the fact. This man had stepped off the comfort of his long life to help them catch a killer – another man who refused to die, one even older than Elspeth. Then, once everything was finished, he had told them a story.

Standing in the darkness of a suburban street, he'd related that in a village called Little Buxberry, there had been a grave which bore the name Jacob Ravens. Ravens was a horror novelist of the 1930s and 1940s, who was well known for dabbling in the actual occult. A sinister figure who moved between planes of reality and seemingly damaged worlds wherever he travelled. But a man who, unlike Elspeth Carmine, had been able to die. Killing himself in a New York hotel room in 1953. However, this particular grave should have been of no interest to them, as the facts suggested that Jacob Ravens had never been buried within it. His body was entombed in California.

It should thus have been a curio, an easy to ignore quirk, but there had been a strange incident in the churchyard just over a year ago.

Apparently, a teenage girl named Alison, had become obsessed with Ravens and his writings. When her computer was later examined, more than a hundred and fifty of his short stories were found downloaded. She had also discovered this grave in St Nicholas's Churchyard and, through interpreting Ravens's writings, had determined a way she thought would restore the man to life. One which, inevitably, involved the spilling of blood. Thus she lured a schoolmate, who himself (entirely coincidentally, as far as anyone could tell they were no relation), possessed the unlucky name of Jake Ravens to the churchyard. Then she had stabbed him. Killed him and left him to bleed on the sod. After which, she had sliced open her wrists and bled to death beside him. In addition, earlier that afternoon she had beaten to death the vicar, hitting him with his own wine bottle. One could only guess she feared he was going to stop her. Or possibly his death was also part of the ritual.

The whole thing was a strange and sad story, one which could be a tragic footnote to Ravens's legacy. Even after seventy years, he continued to be capable of wrecking lives. But there was something else Elspeth told them, which had been borne true by Ludo's further reading of the case notes. The grave itself had been disturbed. And if the investigators at the scene hadn't known better, they'd have thought it was the case of something digging itself free from the earth, rather than Alison (or another unknown party) digging down.

On her laptop, the story Alison had made the most notes on concerned a man who brought his son back to life through the spilling of blood. This seemed to be what Alison was trying to do. She was attempting to reanimate

Jacob Ravens. But there had been nothing at all in the grave. Somehow a stone had been erected, without any body being interred. So if there was nothing there, if no corpse had ever been put under the soil, then what on earth could have dug its way loose?

It was a chilly December morning when Ludo arrived. He had worn his thickest overcoat, and yet felt the bite of frost. This was ridiculous to think of, as Ludo lived these days in Copenhagen. He was used to Scandinavian winters. And yet here he was, being defeated by whatever winter England could offer.

He'd bought a coffee from a very pleasant man at the train station, and strolled the ten-minute walk to St Nicholas's Churchyard. Pleased to see, when he arrived, the gates were open. (It would have been a truly irritating experience if they'd been locked. Yes, he could have used his skeleton keys, but it would seem very bad form to break into Church of England property.) Before he'd left, he'd scoured every document he could find to make sure he'd be able to locate the grave. It was in the far corner, not close to any other plots. But, as it transpired, he needn't have worried. The stone was standing, the surrounding earth had been smoothed and reseeded, but attached to the grave itself was a loose end of yellow police tape fluttering in the breeze. Even if he'd never heard the story, he would have known something untoward had happened there.

Ludo took a seat on the bench nearest the grave and pondered the errant piece of tape. The crimes had taken place more than a year ago. At the time the police departed, it could have been missed. But why had no one in the intervening period untied it? He could only assume no one could bear to. That it was a remembrance itself, and to take it away would remove any sign of what had happened. It would make it appear like any other churchyard in any other village in the country. Undoubtedly, there were those who would want that; who would wish to pretend the incident hadn't happened. But three people had died – a boy, a man and a misguided girl. They had no proper memorial here and nor was there likely to be, but it didn't mean they shouldn't be forgotten. And the little wisp of tape ensured, for the moment, they wouldn't be.

Coffee cooling, Ludo sat and stared. He had no idea what he was looking for, only that it felt important for him to see it. What had been the reason Ravens, or his proxies, had chosen to have this grave mounted? A grave without any remains underneath. Yes, it hadn't taken too much in the way of research to discover this small village was the place Jacob Ravens had grown up. But so what? He had moved to London when he was a teen, toured the globe (this globe, amongst other globes) and eventually settled in America. As far as anyone could tell, he'd never visited Little Buxberry again. Indeed, in the archive, there were letters from his father begging him to visit his sick mother. Letters which didn't seem to have been answered. Little Buxberry, then, hadn't been much on his mind.

It was, of course, his brother who arranged for the grave to be erected here. Although Gerald Ravens comes across in most accounts as a cypher, rather than an actual human being. Those who knew him well couldn't say much about him. He was a non-entity who lived in his younger brother's shadow. So, it seemed unlikely he'd have made these arrangements and erected the grave and interred whatever (or whoever) was buried there, without receiving specific instructions from Jacob Ravens himself before he died.

Which returned the whole thing to *why*.

Ravens's body was buried in California, in a small graveyard near Monterey. Ludo had an alert set up to let him know if it was disturbed in any way, and fellow agent Minako Cohen was on the ground also keeping an ear tuned.

So until something else happened, the only thing he could do was make a pilgrimage to Little Buxberry, and try to get answers to at least one of the questions rampaging through his mind.

But as Ludo sat sipping his lukewarm coffee, someone

else came through the gate. A large man wrapped tight against the cold. He too had a thick black overcoat, and a scarf swathed around the bottom half of his face, so there was only a bit of skin visible beneath a flat cap. He was heavy and walked with both a stoop and a leaden-footed shuffle.

He nodded at Ludo as he entered. They were the only two people in the churchyard in the cold, so it was polite. Then he lingered at the gate, clearly pondering whether he should approach this stranger. He turned and looked along the path leading to the church, and then decided he would go for it, ambling toward the bench.

"Hello!" called Ludo with a smile. As the man got closer, Ludo could see the white square of a vicar's dog collar poking through a gap in the folds of the scarf.

The man nodded, but didn't speak until he was virtually next to Ludo. His voice was high, thin and a little asthmatic. "Hullo to you too."

"Would you care to join me?"

"I can never decide what's more awkward if there's someone else here," the man said, resting his much larger frame beside Ludo. Ludo almost expected the bench to creak. "Whether to come and join the person, or whether to sit on one of the other benches. But then, if there are only two people here, it seems more awkward to be sat at perpendicular walls of the churchyard trying not to meet each other's gazes."

"How do you decide?" asked Ludo.

"Well," the man said in a jocular tone, as if pleased to be asked. "I have decided if they are obviously lost in grief, then I don't join them. Nobody wants that, even if I have a certain expertise in dealing with grief. But if the person in question is a man simply contemplating the day, then I think, why not?"

"Why not, indeed."

"I'm Reverend Bland, by the way."

"Ludo Carstairs."

They shook hands, Ludo's fingers lost in the vicar's giant paw, and then they sat in silence for a good thirty seconds. As if they had exhausted all the things they could possibly say to each other already.

"I suppose you're wondering what that particular piece of decoration is about," said Bland finally, nodding towards the tape. "People do. One day I will have to summon the nerve to untie it, but I haven't got there yet."

Ludo took another sip of coffee. "I'm aware there was a tragedy here."

"Yes, two young people. And my predecessor as well. But between you and me, I feel he may have brought a great deal of what happened to him upon himself. You don't get beaten to death in your own home by a shy teenage girl wielding one of your bottles of wine, unless there is a back story. I mean, he had gold candlesticks inside his home. If she'd wanted a cudgel, then others were available." He blushed under his scarf. "I'm sorry, I shouldn't speak ill of the dead."

"What of the young people?" asked Ludo. "Teenagers, weren't they?"

Reverend Bland nodded sadly. "Mere children."

"I understand they were found over there." Ludo nodded towards the police tape.

"I wonder what went through the young girl's mind that evening." The reverend sighed. "Quite why she behaved the way she did. What was the point of it? I understand adolescents suffer from extreme emotions, and they sometimes have a fascination with death. It would be hard to believe when looking at me today, but I was a similar youth myself. However, most never take it that far. But she took it too far. Very, very far. I'm not sure she meant to kill my predecessor. Probably it was to make him sleep for a while. But I think she meant to kill the boy, or at least to do him horrible harm."

"Any reason she chose that grave?" Ludo asked casually. The coffee cup was at last finished. He placed it on the bench next to him.

The reverend shrugged. "It's simply a grave, as far as I'm aware."

"Really? Is there such a thing as *simply* a grave?" Ludo said. "Graveyards hold a deep fascination for me, and part of it is imagining the hundreds of stories you have within. You get the hard facts on the stone: '*Edward Malpas – 14th February 1925 – 5th November 2005*', but it only tells the baldest of truths. This is someone who lived and loved. They would have thrown tantrums when they were young, danced at weddings, sung in the bathtub, become angry when their football team lost, shown affection to cats and dogs, hugged their kids tight."

"You are quite correct. What is said on a gravestone is a marker, nothing more."

"But the one over there, with the embarrassment of police tape attached to it, that one is *just* a grave, is it?"

A breeze blew past them and both men huddled a little tighter in their coats, the reverend pondering.

"I haven't been here very long, as obviously people weren't expecting what happened to my predecessor to happen, so it took a little while to get me in place. But as far as I'm aware, it's simply a grave. No different from any of the others here. Nothing of interest in there."

"From what I've heard," said Ludo. "There's nothing at all in there anymore, and there shouldn't have been anything in the first place."

The reverend glanced furtively around. "What have you heard?"

A broad smile crossed Ludo Carstairs's face. "Only what you informed me, Elspeth."

Beside him, the reverend gave a shake and a shudder and then emitted a low, avuncular rumble. So different from the voice he'd been using until then. He slowly straightened his frame and pulled the scarf from his face. Then he peeled away a putty nose and a wrinkled chin, and beamed his big smile at Ludo.

He spoke in his proper voice, which was smooth and radio friendly, a transatlantic accent always brimming with good humour, no matter how desperate the situation. "I don't know what I'm more disappointed about, old chap, the fact you saw through my disguise, or the fact it took you so long to see through my disguise."

"It didn't take me too long," said Ludo. "I humoured you for a little while."

"Of course you did. How often do you see a vicar, after all? How often do you meet a vicar who falls amiably into conversation with you? This isn't a Dorothy L. Sayers novel. The whole thing was preposterous to its core."

"What are you doing here, Elspeth?"

"Oh, I imagine I am doing the same as you. I am checking whether anything else is going to dig its way clear of the soil."

They peered together at the corner. Apart from the incongruous strands of police tape, it was such an idyllic-looking spot. It was hard to imagine anything too terrible had happened there.

"Why are you interested, Elspeth?"

"Because I've been hearing things," he said. "I've been listening for them, but they've definitely been there for me to listen to. There is something there. Something strange. Something the likes of me, a denizen of the *demi monde*, realises is strange and knows to be afeard of."

"What is it?"

"Whatever it is which pulled itself from the grave."

"And what's that then?" asked Ludo. "As I still don't truly understand. Is it the ghoulish remains of Jacob Ravens?"

Elspeth laughed and half swivelled on the seat towards him. "I honestly cannot tell if you're joking or not. I think not, but you have a natural facetiousness to you. I don't mind that, as I have it too. It used to be called 'ironical' in my day. We have irony, of course. In fact, it might be a curse of modern life. So many people see the world through an ironic lens. However, 'ironical' isn't a thing young men aspire to in this age. It's not what they aim to make their entire personas. It's a thing which is."

"What are you saying?" asked Ludo.

"I'm saying whatever this is, it has to be dealt with in a manner utterly serious. Whatever has dug itself out of the ground is worth your full and most undivided attention."

Another breeze blew past them both.

"Is this the point," said Ludo, "where you tell me what it is, or at least drop a few cryptic clues to send me in the right general direction?"

Elspeth sighed. "I only wish I could. I don't know what was actually buried there. I can't say how it was possible for whatever it was to come back. Maybe it was Jacob Ravens's heart. If I was writing a melodrama and speculating, it's what I would go for. It was prised from his chest and taken across the Atlantic in a box of ice and buried here without any official record being made. Who knows what ceremony would have taken place when it happened? In the intervening years it has grown, it has developed a whole other body, it has become sentient."

"Interesting theory. But why hasn't the one in California similarly prised itself free? If it's the man's actual body."

"Perhaps it's ready to," said Elspeth. "But conditions haven't been right there for the final push. After all, how many graves have fresh warm blood spread across them?" He gave a shudder. "Spine-tingling, isn't it? I tremble in the middle of the night."

"But why have you come here now?" asked Ludo.

"You are here too. What is the attraction for you?"

Ludo demurred. "You've met succubi. You've presumably met vampires and other creatures of the *demi monde*, as you put it. What is it about this one which makes you so anxious?"

There was a good minute when Elspeth Carmine didn't answer. Which, for such a normally loquacious man, seemed to stretch to half an hour short of eternity.

"Because those others you mention, are part of the natural order of things," he said at last. "Yes, yes, the average man on the street doesn't believe in vampires and there is no reason why he should have his mind troubled by such things. Vampires are not, in the main, disrupters. But this, whatever this is, is different. It shouldn't be here. And whatever it's doing, it almost certainly shouldn't be doing it."

"So that's why you're pretending to be a vicar in this churchyard?"

"Ha!" exclaimed Elspeth at the top of his voice. "I was merely play-acting a vicar for you. To amuse myself, to see how long it took you to notice. But yes, I have been keeping an eye on this place. And when I realised you were coming, I thought this was as good a time as any to renew our acquaintance."

"How did you realise I was coming?" asked Ludo.

Elspeth smiled inscrutably. "I can trust you to look into this, can't I, Carstairs?" he said. "You will give it your best."

"Of course."

"You're a good man. And if I had to have anyone handling this, it would be you and Garris. I met him once."

"Who?" asked Ludo. Knowing very well Elspeth Carmine wasn't referring to Garris.

"Jacob Ravens." Elspeth smiled. "The real breathing Jacob Ravens. He and his absolutely delightful wife. It was at a do for Literary London in Fitzrovia. At the end of my career and, I suppose, the beginning of his. I didn't warm to him, however," he said with a sniff. "Undoubtedly I could see he was handsome and charming, but equally there was something in his manner quite repellent. I found him a very vain man. To my tastes, he seemed duplicitous. But he didn't scare me on that occasion. This thing he might have become, however, *it* scares me."

The police tape fluttered once more in the breeze.

Ludo leant into him. "If you are here watching the grave, what are you watching for?"

"I told you, I want to see if anything else comes out of it."

"And if it does?"

"I appreciate you and Garris have left me be, and I *do* appreciate it. But other agents from your aptly named Organisation have occasionally made themselves a nuisance around London, trying to track me down. I don't blame them. You are a bureaucracy. And much as any bureaucracy, you have to have your damn forms stamped. That's why I've taken this brief break to the countryside. But if I saw something here. Or if there was anything else which indicated the presence of this new Ravens, then I would scream from the top of my lungs and bring every one of you boys to my side. I wouldn't care what happened to my safety from that point on."

He stood up. No longer stooped and heavy-footed. Instead, a tall and spry man.

"Besides which, I wanted to talk to you. It's been lovely catching up, Carstairs."

"Likewise."

"Best of luck. I have a feeling you're going to need it."

CHAPTER ONE

There are so many vampires in Las Vegas.

All night-time cities have their bloodsuckers, be it New York, Rio, Mexico City, Macau, Madrid, Paris, or London. But Vegas seemed particularly populous with them. No vampire wants to find him or herself stuck in a sleepy town, where everyone is tucked in bed by eleven-thirty. Their night-time activities will draw attention in such a place. Better to mix with those who want to party, as well as the insomniacs, and the warm-blooded people who – through their own pursuits – love the darkness.

In the main, vampires are careful with their behaviours. It's only in books and movies where they're blood-crazed fiends draining every passing maiden. In reality, vampires don't want to be hunted down and staked through the heart by a modern-day Van Helsing. Smart vampires do pretty much what they always did, and make arrangements. They take a pint of blood from the neck of a willing victim (or several willing victims), every couple of nights. Each big city with a thriving nightlife has vampires, but they also have vampire groupies. People who enjoy the knowledge that they have an intimate connection with one of the undead, even if most of the rest of the world will never believe them.

It means vampires get their sustenance, and their fans get their secret story, while the stake-wielders and garlic-carriers of the Twenty-First Century are kept at bay.

That's the way it seemed to be with the tall, pale man who this evening stood in front of me at one of the roulette tables of *Circus-Circus* on the Las Vegas strip. A long-dead individual, who still went by his human name of Yardsmith.

We had a file on him at the London Headquarters of The Organisation, but the fact it was so thin suggested he had behaved himself across the century of his existence. As far as we could tell, he had been in Vegas for decades, but there had been no reports of any rampages. Or at least none which could be connected to him. No, he was a vampire who truly understood self-preservation. Of course, as myth tells us, they are creatures who revel in danger and excitement. And maybe it was the sublimation of those urges which explained why he had placed a thousand dollars on the number thirteen.

It didn't explain much else of this night, though.

Why exactly we found ourselves there, for instance.

A message had arrived through trusted channels at The Organisation, saying this Yardsmith wanted to speak to us. He wanted to speak to my partner, Ludo Carstairs, in particular. It was strange, yet intriguing enough we had to find him. But as he stood at the roulette wheel, painfully thin, with a beautiful young woman on his arm (who I could only guess gave her neck every couple of nights), there was nothing to suggest a creature of the night with such an important message.

Circus-Circus is the last whiff of old Las Vegas still standing on the main strip. These days, most of the hotels and casinos are big corporate behemoths, whose character had been expensively bought and designed. *Circus-Circus* is the real thing, a circus flavoured casino (of course) whose run-down seediness has a lot more character than any of the paintings of clowns adorning its walls. It's the casino Sean Connery, as James Bond, visits in *Diamonds Are Forever*; while if you want another film reference, the real-life gangster Joe Pesci played in *Casino* ran his operation out of there for a time. It is dark and atmospheric, and it's where we found this vampire who was trying to get in touch with us,

From what we knew, Cole Yardsmith had been a vampire in Vegas since the 1970s. He therefore must have remembered *Circus-Circus* in something approaching its prime, which probably explained his attachment to it. Everyone there seemed to know him. The croupier gave him a warm smile, while one of the waiters trotted by and asked if he'd like a drink. He had said yes, which was interesting as vampires can't drink any liquids apart from blood, but it must have been for his lady companion. Some of the gamblers looked at his wager, not with shock, but with a sense that this had happened before.

Sometime in the 1980s, Yardsmith had started dressing in what was then an approximation of a rock star. Tight leather trousers and snakeskin coat; the velvet shirt he wore underneath unbuttoned halfway down his bony chest. His dirty blond hair was spiked upwards and backwards, while in the night-time dark of the casino, he kept his thick-rimmed sunglasses on.

To be fair, he had the right frame for an androgynous rock star. And it wasn't as if he was going to put weight on. According to what we had on file, he was changed sometime after the First World War. He was a veteran of the conflict and only twenty-one years old, when his destiny was forever altered. His body was long, lithe and angular. There wasn't much muscle on him, but there wasn't any fat. It was the same with his face. His cheekbones were sharp and left the cheeks below with a hollowed appearance. The effect was, in later years, called *junkie chic*. But for him, it was what being poor and hungry in 1919 looked like. Similarly, his teeth had the ratty aspect of someone who'd taken far too much smack, but was a reflection of the dentistry available to him when he was breathing. Vampires only display their fangs when they come in for a kill, and I thought how strange those long incisors would be alongside the worn-down bluntness of the rest of his mouth.

I watched him as the wheel spun. Making my observations a short distance from the table, as I didn't have the money to place my own bet. The ball landed on number thirty-eight, rather than thirteen. Yardsmith didn't appear downhearted, however. He placed another thousand on thirteen and waited for it to spin again. Eventually, of course, that number would come up, but I wondered if he seriously had the funds to wait for it to happen.

The woman beside him tittered encouragingly, clearly thrilled by his risk-taking.

If I had to guess, I'd say she was no more than twenty-one. Undoubtedly, she had the looks of a stereotypical rock star girlfriend. Blow-dried black locks teased to an almost unfeasible degree. Thick black eye-liner and bright red lipstick, and a tight white dress which left little to the imagination. It showed off her curves (possibly surgically enhanced), and also the fact she didn't have an ounce of fat on her. I considered whether she might be a vampire as well. Even if vampires are territorial creatures who don't appreciate competition, surprising things can happen. They do occasionally hook up. But the only thing she had on which wasn't white was the black choker around her neck, and I guessed it was to hide the bite marks. Vampires don't feed off each other.

For now, I kept my distance and watched. The message had been received from Yardsmith, and after some discussion, we had been dispatched. He wasn't aware we were coming tonight. I suppose he had no way of knowing whether his message was being acted upon. He hadn't entered the casino displaying any nervousness. He didn't stare around to see if anyone was awaiting him. Instead, he'd strutted in. Suggesting this was already a good night, and he intended to make it better. I guess a gambler, be they human or creature of the undead, always carries a certain amount of confidence with them.

Half-a-dozen players had gathered around the roulette wheel, and I stood in the shadows behind them. Tall enough to see over their heads, but inconspicuous enough, Yardsmith wasn't immediately going to spot I was staring at him. There were others watching the wheel, and I positioned myself as one of them. I was another guy with a half-drunk bottle of Michelob in hand, summoning the nerve to have a flutter.

Again the wheel went around, and again Yardsmith was unlucky. There was a little curse under his breath this time, but another chip for a thousand dollars was retrieved from his jacket pocket and he placed in on number thirteen. The girl beside him squealed. The two of them were nothing if not consistent.

"Mr Yardsmith bets!" called the croupier, to raise excitement levels in what was a soporific crowd. It was past midnight and a lot of these people would have been breathing casino air for the last twelve hours.

Yardsmith grinned his ratty grin and appreciated the attention. He raised his hand to acknowledge a cheer which never actually materialised.

One player across the table from him, however, slipped his own chips onto number thirteen as well. It was a smaller amount, only two hundred dollars (which, to me, still seemed a hell of a lot to wager on the spin of a wheel). Yardsmith peered over the table at him and the two men regarded each other. Then Yardsmith nodded once, a gesture which seemed to be both an appreciation for the confidence handed over, and a wishing of good luck.

Everyone else who was interested placed their own bets. But of course, none were as big as Yardsmith's.

Then the croupier blew on the ball and spun it on the wheel. It clattered around. I'd like to say there was an expectant hush. That everyone waited anxiously to see if Yardsmith, as well as his new friend from across the table, would finally get lucky with number thirteen. But that would be to overstate things. We watched, absolutely, but most of those watching were more intent on their own bets than on Yardsmith's. And those with an idle curiosity, a category which as far as anyone could tell included me, kept an eye on the biggest bet, but didn't care much either way.

The ball bounced into its final resting place.

Number thirteen!

Yardsmith had done it!

His friend across the table had picked the right time to back him.

On his arm, Yardsmith's companion screamed with delight. She bounced up and down beside him, which in her sheer white dress got a lot more attention than anything which had happened at the roulette wheel. The two of them hugged and, with his big ratty grin, Yardsmith swooped in to claim his winnings. Letting them rattle into his jacket pocket. Possibly he was going to head off elsewhere and try his luck at another game, but clearly he'd done his bit on roulette tonight.

Of course, the man across the table had his own smaller pile of winnings. He retrieved them more carefully and delicately than Yardsmith, and placed them neatly into his own coat pocket. Then, much the same as Yardsmith had done, he detached himself from the table.

He headed towards the vampire.

I made my move as well.

"I wanted to say," said the little man, in his posh English accent. "You looked exceptionally lucky then, which is why I backed you."

Yardsmith and his date had both turned around to peer at the man with almost matching indulgent smiles – except hers was whiter and prettier.

"No problem at all," said Yardsmith, in tones which were harsher than one might have imagined. Maybe he had smoked a couple of lifetime's worth of cigarettes. "But given what was happening to me before you came on board, it's you who's the lucky one."

"Are you British?" asked the girlfriend.

The man smiled at her and then at Yardsmith, just as I reached his shoulder.

"Indeed I am," he said. "My name is Ludo Carstairs. And this is Michael Garris."

I nodded.

Ludo's name earned a gasp from the young woman. Yardsmith gawped for a few seconds before managing a smile, which came more from anxiety than anywhere else.

"Carstairs, are you?" he said. "If so, you're the man I wanted to see."

CHAPTER TWO

"You received a message from me, didn't you?" Yardsmith said. "You were told I had interesting information for you and I would only hand it to you personally. That's what you heard, wasn't it? Well, from my side, I was instructed to wait for your arrival. But to be honest, I was hoping you wouldn't come."

"What do you mean?" asked Ludo.

The vampire grinned his slightly rotted smile. "I had to make myself available, and the best way to do so was to come to the casino every evening. I was given a bankroll to play with. A substantial bankroll. And I could keep using it for as long as I kept making myself available. Do you think I can afford to enjoy myself in such a fashion with my own resources? Of course not. But with the bankroll, Marcia and I have had a good few weeks of joy with the wheel, the dice and all the other entertainments this fine city has to offer." He squeezed his companion's thigh. "I haven't been this happy in decades."

"So you're the bait in the trap?" I asked.

"Yes, sir." His darkly intense eyes fixed me. "But I'm very happy bait."

We'd retired to the hotel bar. A place which, even by the

standards of a Vegas hotel, was all shadows. If you came in at twelve noon, you'd almost certainly feel exactly the same ambience as we did in the early hours. We had taken four leather chairs around a small round table in the far corner. The bar had been pretty much empty when we arrived, which meant we immediately got the attention of the mini-skirted waitress. Yardsmith didn't order anything. Not even treating himself to a glass of water he could pretend to sip. Marcia asked for a Twisted Tequila Sunrise, which turned out to be a cocktail of dark liquid floating on top of volcanic red. As she'd sat next to Yardsmith, she'd met us both in the eye, and said with a certain earnestness: "I *know* what he is." Making it clear we could talk openly in front of her. Both Ludo and I stayed safe on lemonades. Not quite buying into the "*what happens in Vegas, stays in Vegas*" vibe.

"What do you know of us?" I asked.

He gave a chuckle from deep in his throat. "I've heard of The Organisation. I'm aware you investigate the strange and uncanny. I've concluded that it's the best thing for beings such as me *not* to draw your attention."

"And yet you did?"

"I like money. I enjoy gambling and I love pretty women. It's been a fun ride."

Beside him, Marcia simpered, whilst not losing her sense of earnestness.

"So, what's the message?" asked Ludo.

"I'm sorry?"

"What do you have to impart to me? Why have I come all this way?"

Yardsmith shifted a little uncomfortably in his seat, and Marcia took the chance to put her hand on his leg, squeezing reassuringly. "That's the stupid and embarrassing thing I have to admit to you. I don't actually know. I was ordered to wait until you came, but I do not know what the message is." He ran his fingers through his hair. "As you said, I'm bait in the trap. The bait is very rarely made privy to the overarching plan."

"Okay then," said Ludo. "What do we do? What is supposed to happen now I've shown up?"

Yardsmith fished an older model iPhone from his pocket. But reluctantly. I guessed that the good times of the last few weeks were slipping away. "I am supposed to send a message."

"Who to?"

"The person who employed me. My benefactor of the past few weeks."

"Who is?" I asked.

"I'd rather not say. Or rather I've been instructed not to say. They want to be the ones who tell you."

"Okay," said Ludo. "Do you want to get on with doing that then?"

Yardsmith nodded and gave another glimpse of his unpleasant smile, before typing a couple of words into the screen and hitting send.

We all sat awkwardly for a minute, as if in the mistaken belief the response would be instantaneous, and then with a shared disappointment when it wasn't. Those of us who could drink normal drinks all took a sip.

It was Ludo who broke the silence. "I appreciate you may not have been involved in the planning stage, but what do you *think* happens next?"

Yardsmith swallowed. "The information I have is that a van will pick us up. Pick *all of us* up. Apparently we all have to go together to the destination, and then the message will be imparted. Once I've delivered you, and it's confirmed *it is you*, then I get my last payment."

"It's like she doesn't trust you." Marcia shook her head disapprovingly, hand on his knee. "Like she believes you're going to try to smuggle an imposter past her."

He shot her a glare, which Marcia didn't appear to notice, at so carelessly giving away the gender of his benefactor.

Not that the information helped us much.

Ludo reclined in his leather chair and steepled his

fingers. The waitress seemed to take this as a sign we might want more drinks, despite what we'd ordered last time being largely untouched in front of us. We thanked her politely, and then Ludo waited until she was out of earshot:

"I'm supposed to accompany a vampire, who does not have the message I was promised, to a random location somewhere? Do you know if the next stop is in Nevada? Or is it farther afield?"

Yardsmith shrugged.

"Once there," Ludo continued, "the lady who is your employer, will presumably pass me this now long-awaited message. Or, I suppose, given we'll be lost in the middle of nowhere, she could do anything to us."

"We could all be taken somewhere we don't return from," I said.

The notion offended Yardsmith. "I'm one of the good guys! I have taken this job on good faith. I do not expect any harm to happen to anybody."

"And yet you find yourself caught in something deliberately opaque and mysterious," Ludo said. "Tell me, how have you become involved in this?"

He signed. "Because of money, of course. I'm more than a hundred years old and I am not built to hold down a regular job. I am a vampire and thus hardly a creature of the nine-to-five. Those jobs which exist in the darkness, require you to interview in the day. Besides at night-time, I have other needs." Yardsmith squeezed Marcia's hand in his lap. She simpered in response.

"You seem to have that sorted," Ludo observed.

"As best I can, but as lovely as Marcia is, I can't feed on her every night. I'd make her ill or I'd kill her. We are companions and we live together and she looks after my other needs. But I need fresh blood as well. And Marcia helps me with that."

"I've built a network," she said.

"I don't kill anyone!" he told us vehemently. "I have killed people, as I was a soldier in a war a long time ago. But

I haven't killed anyone since I turned. I promise you. I've been an exemplary example of my breed. However, I can't work and I am lacking in funds. I burned through what meagre life savings I had a century ago. Yet reality dictates that I have to pay the rent on an apartment, I need food for my companion, as well as make-up and clothes to ensure she is at her most beautiful."

"I'm simply happy to be with you!" Marcia said, with eyes wide and a tone which wasn't entirely convincing.

He smiled at her and then looked at us. "I need wheels in this land of the automobile. Plus, I take pleasure in buying silk shirts and I enjoy gambling."

"And cleaning the pool," she added.

"Yes. So it all adds up when you don't have any money."

"And I'm guessing," I said, "what you're being paid for this, on top of the amount you've already gambled, means you're going to squash any qualms about getting into a van with no idea where you're heading?"

"I trust my employer." He clenched his jaw. "I believe what she has told me. I am going to bring you to her, and then I will be paid enough to eliminate all my debts. Enough for me to be secure for another decade. In ten years' time, I may have gambled it all. I might indeed be in the same position. But for now, I am delighted at the prospect of the worry disappearing. Of those red notices which come through the door turning a friendlier colour."

"What if we don't come with you?" I ventured.

"Why wouldn't you?" Marcia responded. "You've come all this way already."

"But you know who you're working for," Ludo said. "You have that amount of information, at least. Besides which, and I don't mean to come off unnecessarily rude here, but it's not – as I'm sure you can appreciate – the safest course for us to trust the word of a vampire and his familiar. Neither of whom we've ever laid eyes on before. Particularly when you've behaved so enigmatically."

"We prefer the word 'consort' to 'familiar'," he told us.

"A familiar is, as I'm sure you understand, a kind of servant. A long time ago, when I was first getting used to my new self, I met the man who Bram Stoker allegedly based Renfield on – and that is not who Marcia is at all."

"I apologise," Ludo said.

"It's okay," said Marcia. "Because of the accent, you English can always get away with being ruder than we can."

"Ludo makes a fair point, however," I said. "Why should we trust you? How can we be sure this ride in a van isn't the last journey we ever take?"

"I don't think it's going to be like that."

"You don't *think*?" Ludo's eyebrow arched.

Yardsmith held his hands in front of him. "I'm not going to swear my employer is a good person. The one time I met her, I was made distinctly uncomfortable. There is something unsettling about her. Even to those such as me. What I have grasped, however, is there is purpose to her actions. She has an agenda. And I don't think the agenda is to kill you with no good reason. She wouldn't have paid me an emperor's ransom, or dragged you around the world, to commit an act so crude. She could have had you killed in England, if that was her wish."

"Could she?" I asked.

"Yes. Do not underestimate my employer's reach. I don't think she is going to harm you, because why would she? Just as I don't believe she is going to stiff me for my cash. I know she has it, so why leave the mess?"

"Is that the main issue for you?" asked Ludo. "Not whether Garris or I survive, but whether you get your payment."

The vampire put one finger in front of his lips and pondered the question. "I wouldn't like to think I was working for a murderer," he said finally "She might make me uncomfortable, but I believe she is more civilised than *that*. As I understand it, the message is one she wants to utter to you with her own lips. She doesn't want to put herself out there for you to find, so she's using me. I'm a poor, broke, old bloodsucker. I'm easy to use. The message will be imparted, I will get my money, and we can both do what we wish with what we've received."

"Why don't you tell us this lady's name?" asked Ludo.

He shook a little. Unusual, as vampires didn't normally feel the cold.

"That is not my place to say," he said. "I have a narrow scope and I intend to stay within it. A sizeable sum of cash rests on me doing exactly what has been dictated. And I don't want to jeopardise things by deviating in any way."

He retrieved his phone from his pocket. It had vibrated. He glanced at us, shyly – like an adolescent who isn't sure whether the girl he fancies will go on a date with him. "The van is downstairs. It must have already been close by. I'm conscious, with each passing minute, dawn gets nearer. I'd obviously prefer to have this done by dawn. So, shall we go?"

I turned to Ludo. Although knowing him as I did, I could guess what his choice was going to be.

"Why not?" he said, with a smirk. "It might be fun. And I have always wanted to go on a Magical Mystery Tour."

CHAPTER THREE

Of course, the chances of it being a trap were high, but in the basement garage of *Circus-Circus*, the four of us climbed with no obvious hesitation into the rear of an anonymous looking white van. Its paintwork was stained by the Nevada desert. All of its windows were blacked out, not a ray of sunlight was going to sneak in. For which the vampire would be eternally grateful.

The driver was an older gentleman, with white hair and a trim moustache. There was, however, an obvious hardness to him. He wore a dapper pin-striped suit, which was tailored to his wide frame, but was seventy years away from fashion.

"How far is the drive?" asked Yardsmith. "I *need* to be home by sunrise."

The chauffeur (or butler, or whatever he was) didn't answer him. He gave no sign of being aware he had a vampire in the backseat. Despite this car evidently having been fitted to ferry a vampire.

Marcia sat next to her love, with Ludo and I both facing them and riding backwards. Again her hand was on his thigh.

"It's okay," she said. "Nothing is going to happen to *us*."

He smiled thin-lipped at her, but didn't seem convinced. If I'm honest, I shared some of his nervousness.

Ludo appeared quite relaxed. There was a smile on his face, and his entire posture was of a laid-back expectation. If he'd had a beach towel tucked under his arm, it wouldn't have been too incongruous.

"Why do you think your employer made contact with *you*?" asked Ludo. "Beyond your financial woes, why choose you for this task?"

"I can't say," he said. "I can't say how she heard my name. People in the know knew who I am. And those in the know undoubtedly understood my straitened circumstances. So when it came to someone who was willing to be bait to attract you…"

"A creature of the night." Marcia's words were romantic, but her tone was on edge.

"Yes, darling, that's right. Obviously they thought of me." He shifted uncomfortably. "I appreciate you coming with us now, and I understand you have no reason to trust me. I'm not sure I quite trust it myself. All I can think of is it would be much more work to betray and kill everybody, than to carry through with promises made. But then I've been wrong before. Look at me, I'm a goddamn vampire, I'm an advert for being wrong in the past."

"What do you mean?" asked Ludo.

"Most vampires we've encountered are boastful of their existences," I said.

He sighed, and I realised – since he didn't breathe – it must be an affectation he had given himself. To make him seem a little more human.

"In movies and plays and books, they portray vampires as without souls. They say we are inhuman monsters in thrall to our desires. Well, I have a soul. I laugh, I sing and I have fallen in love. Although my nerve endings are dead, I feel deeply to my non-beating heart."

"I love him too," said Marcia, seeming younger than she was. The two of them held each other's gazes. It was almost, but not quite, touching.

We turned off the main highway, onto a bumpy desert road.

"I've lived a long life," Yardsmith said. "Of course I've had companions before, but nothing compared to what I feel now. And I genuinely worship her. She is my treasure, the rose in my hand. But I can't sit to eat a meal with her. I can't drink with her in any bar. Of course, I can't go for an afternoon stroll with her. I can't" – he hesitated – "make love to her."

She squeezed his hand tight and said in a tone which was half apology and half encouragement: "We've been through that, darling. I don't mind. I really don't. You do other things for me."

"I take your blood is what I do for you. I take your blood and I send you to get what I need. I pile the bills high and ask you to do distasteful work."

Her eyes fixed levelly on Ludo and me, appealing to us to be convinced by her words. "He makes me feel the most beautiful and desired creature alive. He recites poetry from memory. He is a wonderful storyteller, and when he recounts the tales of his life, I am positively in awe. He has shown me an aspect of the world which I'd only been able to dream of. He is the most incredible of creatures and makes me feel lucky to be with him."

"So yours is a love story then?" asked Ludo.

"Yes!" she said.

He nodded. "Absolutely. I have made my home hers and I want to keep it over both our heads. No priest is going to marry us, but I consider us husband and wife."

"What about a late night Elvis impersonator?" I asked.

He seemed affronted, although I hadn't meant my question flippantly. "Do you imagine a man of my vintage would consider a skinny hillbilly who caterwauls a singer?"

"We can be husband and wife in our hearts," she said. "We don't need a piece of paper. We don't need the permission of a man who speaks for a god that does not exist."

Ludo reached into his pocket and retrieved one of his business cards. A quite elegant example, made of thick cream card and with embossed text seemingly formed by an old-fashioned typewriter. Of course it didn't have the name of The Organisation on it. Nor did it have Ludo's own name. Instead, it read 'S. Sparrow', and quoted a random mobile number. He reached across the rear of the van and handed it to Yardsmith.

"Should you make your way through your payment quicker than you anticipate," he said. "Please give us a call. This number will reach me. Eventually."

"Really?" asked Yardsmith.

Which, I'll be honest, was my sentiment too.

"We can't afford to pay anything close to what you're receiving from your mysterious benefactor," continued Ludo. "But we offer consultancy fees. There is a discretionary fund we can dip into when someone passes us valuable information."

"But what valuable information could I possibly provide you with?"

Ludo smiled. "Vampire stuff. How a fellow vampire behaves in a certain circumstance, what we can expect him or her to do. Things of note in the vampire community."

Across the rear seats, Yardsmith's eyes narrowed. "Are you asking me to rat out my kind?"

"No, not at all. Not unless they're doing something which needs to be stopped. We both know, when a vampire starts doing something which needs to be stopped, then if it's not stopped, it becomes very messy. Once suspicion is there, then it becomes difficult for *all* vampires in a city. From what you've said, I don't get the impression you want to move on from Vegas. Certainly you don't want to be chased from the town because of the activities of another."

"No, we don't." Marcia squeezed her lover tighter.

"But, if I'm honest," Ludo said, "I'm thinking more of general information. Whether you have something which will be worth serious money to us, only time will tell. It seems to take a lot to get serious money from The Organisation. Certainly neither I nor Garris have ever managed it. But you can't be certain what will happen along the line. Maybe you can find something which has value for us, but isn't as risky as what you're engaged in tonight."

Ludo turned and glanced at me and there must have been an expression on my face which betrayed my thoughts on this.

"Relax, Garris," he said. "This is a love story."

The chauffer had driven us onto a winding one-track road. I peered around and could determine a large mansion in the distance. Sitting in nothing but desert. The only thing for miles. From when we'd left the Vegas strip, the man hadn't altered his speed at any point, which meant we bounced around in the back. Yardsmith already looked distinctly pale (and not the paleness which is a vampire's natural pallor), but now Marcia joined him. I felt a certain queasiness too.

Yardsmith couldn't actually vomit, but the vampire had other things to concern him.

The sun was starting its creep above the horizon when we pulled up outside the mansion.

Ludo spun around in his seat and addressed the driver. The first time any of us had done so since we left Vegas.

"Excuse me!" he said. "As I'm sure you know, our companion here has a medical condition, which means it's truly inadvisable for him to come into contact with daylight. I assume the coverings on these windows will filter all rays?"

At first it didn't seem the driver was going to answer us, that he was going to sit there silently and pretend he didn't understand English. But then, at the point Ludo was going to reach through and tap his shoulder, the man's voice snapped with irritation at us:

"My employer is well aware of your friend's *condition*. Proper arrangements have, of course, been made." His accent was strange. Transatlantic. As if it had started off

British, but had spent years and years in The States. "These coverings on the window will indeed protect him from the sunlight. In addition, I understand his apartment complex has an underground carpark. I am instructed to drive him to the lowest level of it and then make sure he reaches the elevator. Although, if he would rather not risk leaving the vehicle at all while the sun is shining, I have been ordered to leave the van with him and he can stay in it all day."

They both gave a sigh of relief (I wondered if Yardsmith practised different types of sighs), then the vampire nodded in thanks.

As Ludo reached for the door handle, Yardsmith crunched himself as far as he could from the gap. Although the sun was only faintly peeking over the horizon, he wasn't going to take any chances.

Ludo opened the door, and the coldness of the dawn surprised me. Despite being aware – at a conscious level – that temperatures in deserts drop at night-time, I think my body was constantly unprepared for the fact. I yanked my coat tighter around me, and at the same time squinted at the light. It felt far brighter than it should have done. The sun wasn't properly up yet, but the white marble house in front of us seemed to draw every molecule of light towards it. Every ray from the spectrum working to increase the brilliance of its shiny white edifice. At noon, it probably shone like a lost star. But even at this hour, it glowed.

The second we were both through the car door, Marcia slid it shut with a slam behind us. The chauffeur didn't wait. Within moments, the engine was purring, and the van was making its way back along the winding, unpaved desert road.

We had been left there.

Ludo turned around and stared at it ruefully.

"What have we got ourselves into?" I asked.

He shrugged. "It's the type of thing we're always getting ourselves into."

"No. This is the type of thing where you wonder

whether you might not have been better off with the vampire."

Despite not making its departure at high speed, the van had billowed a cloud of red Nevada dust. We squinted and patted it off ourselves. Knowing no matter what we did, there were going to be stains on our dark suits until the next dry cleaning. Then we took in this strange, isolated house.

It spiralled into the air. A tower built to a wide living-space at the top, so the whole thing resembled a glimmering letter T left in the desert. On top of the tower itself, was a house which appeared to be two of three stories high (it was hard to be sure from down below). The house had a lot of windows, and on either side of it stretched out flat open areas which I could only presume were patios.

There was a large and ominous black door at the ground level, but the fact there were no windows next to it almost gave the impression it was a servant's entrance. (Although, given we'd been summoned without a "please" or any explanation, it was probably the door for us.) More promising was that around the tower wound a marble staircase. Going all the way to the house. It looked like it was supposed to be the main entrance. But it also seemed it'd be an absolute joy to climb when the sun had properly emerged.

"What do you reckon?" asked Ludo. "It's obviously a bizarre folly, with its own strange story, but when would you date it? 1950s? 1960s?"

"I haven't a clue," I said.

"It resembles a monument to someone in organised crime. A hide for them, to make sure they were never caught. The home of a man who was too damn careful to be caught. There are no windows in the tower on the way up, so there are no doubt plenty of places to hide within it. While the top floors not only let you enjoy the view, but to see anything coming from miles around. This is a wonderful location to cut yourself off in. A fantastic place to make sure no one sneaks up on you."

I smiled at him. "Do you think the gangster is still at home?"

"Let's hope not," said Ludo. "But keep an eye peeled for tommy guns, just in case."

The heat was starting to build, as the sun's rays shone over the hills. A latent humidity rose from beneath our feet. I hoped, when we finally got in there, the house had air conditioning.

"Shall we?" he asked.

He ignored the big door before us and instead started to ascend the winding staircase. There had to be about a hundred steps in total. They were each three feet long, which meant you had to take two steps for each one. I was glad I was doing this before the sun was full in the sky.

As it was, we each took a little breather when we reached the top.

We found ourselves on a roof terrace. To the left side of the tower, there was a small pool, carved into the heavy marble floor, with pristine chlorinated water. Black sun loungers were placed around. They showed stains of sand, but appeared new. A four feet high white wall was built around the edge, and there was a glass of red wine resting atop it. The glass was three quarters full and was the only indication that this wasn't a completely empty house.

Ahead of us, we could peer through the floor-length windows into the house itself. It was grey inside and tastefully appointed, if somewhat Spartan. There were two sofas and a coffee table facing into the terrace, while behind was a large shiny kitchen and a dining area, before another set of windows and the second terrace beyond. There were no plants of any description. Not even cacti.

Ludo stood in front of the closed glass door and put his hand on the handle.

He looked at me and winked. "We came all this way…"

Then he pushed the handle, and the door creaked open. We stepped into the fortunately cool air within.

And as we did, from a distance, an old gramophone

record started playing. From it came the croaky, warbling voice of an old folk singer:

"There were three ravens sat on a tree,
Down a down,
Hey down, hey down,
There were three ravens sat on a tree,
With a down,
There were three ravens sat on a tree,
They were as black as they might be.
With a down, derrie, derrie, derrie, down, down.
The one of them said to his mate,
Where shall we our breakfast take?"

The two of us froze as we listened to it.

Then at the end of the first refrain, Ludo called: "Hello!"

But there was no response. The record continued playing.

CHAPTER FOUR

We took two steps inside, in the vague direction of the music, and then stopped. The record finished, and we heard the click and the whirr of the arm swinging from the disc. That left the hum of an air conditioning unit, but nothing else.

'*Mausoleum*' was the word which came to mind. We had been taken by a member of the undead to a place of the actual dead. There was nothing alive here. Nothing could grow in the desert outside, and in this house there was apparently nothing moving anymore. Only a recording pressed in vinyl long ago, and sung by a presumably long-dead singer.

Yet someone had put the record on. Someone had, until recently, been enjoying a glass of red wine outside.

I hunted around for any other vague, but tell-tale, signs of life. The kitchen had a shiny new kettle, coffee machine, toaster and a microwave. But there was nothing else on the surfaces. No crumbs or stains or spills. There was no indication anyone had recently cooked in here. It was the same with the sofas facing onto the patio where we'd entered. There was no indentations in any of the cushions. No hint of disruption. The whole set-up could have been delivered from the furniture warehouse and unwrapped from its plastic in the last three hours.

It was akin to a show house. And then again, not really. A show house is empty and unlived in, but those selling it go to the effort of making it appear habitable. There are fresh flowers and, if they're really trying hard, the smell of baking bread. This place was cold, empty and unwelcoming.

"Do you want me to look downstairs?" I asked. "Inside the tower. Try to find the person who invited us?"

Ludo almost framed "yes", but then stopped himself as the word formed on his lips. He had seen something outside. On the other, larger patio, which was starting to be hit properly by the morning's rays.

I followed his gaze and saw it too. There was a woman lying face down on a sun-lounger, wearing a one piece black swimsuit. Her arms were outstretched, giving the impression she was enjoying blistering sunshine, despite the fact we were a good hour or two from that being possible. Her head was nearest to us; her hair was dark and thick and hung in curls over her shoulders. Without yet seeing her face, it was obvious she was young, lithe and attractive.

Good manners suggested we shouldn't creep up on a young woman lying prone in a swimsuit, even if she had gone to ridiculous efforts to bring us into her home. Ludo therefore made sure to rattle the lock on the sliding doors between us. She was going to be aware we were coming.

Not that she peered in our direction, or moved in any way. There wasn't a tensing of a single muscle at our approach. Instead she remained still.

For a second, I thought she might be dead. That we'd arrived too late to meet our hostess. Maybe her body was a macabre welcoming gift for us.

We stepped into the growing heat, wondering if we were going to have to check her pulse. But then a posh English voice rang out:

"Ah, there you are! I was beginning to suspect I was going to have to fund the vampire's gambling habit for the next ten years."

She pushed herself onto her elbows to stare at us. I tried and failed not to take a sharp intake of breath. She was stunning. Genuinely beautiful. A cherubic Mediterranean goddess, who could have been a film star or a model. Her shining dark brown eyes peered at us with a fresh faced look of inquisition, a heavy ruby necklace dangling from her neck.

Ludo had taken a gasp as well.

"You're Emilia Ravens!" he said.

The woman on the sun lounger made no movement, nor did she reply to what he said. But her stillness seemed an affirmation.

"You're Jacob Ravens's widow!"

CHAPTER FIVE

Jacob Ravens was a pulp horror author of the 1930s and 1940s. In his day, he was surprisingly popular and enjoyed a successful career. In the years since, however, he has largely been forgotten by the wider public. Except for a small, but dedicated cult, of fans. Amongst this group, there were those of such fervour, they firmly believed that when he was writing his horror fantasies concerning other worlds and alternative planes of existence, he wasn't creating fictions, he was describing something utterly true which had happened to him. He was writing from his own experiences and thus, everything in his wild and outrageous stories was a chronicle of reality.

To most people, this would seem the type of hysterical nonsense which frequently goes on in the most shadowy corners of the internet. The rational-minded who heard these deductions, would be incredulous to the point of amazement. But that's exactly the way we at The Organisation liked it. What we'd known for a long time was there was more than a little truth to these beliefs. Ravens had not merely been an author, he had been the darkest of magicians – and he had bent the surrounding reality to suit his purposes.

Not long ago, Ludo and I had handled a matter in a manor house in Ireland, and it was a long-lost work by Jacob Ravens which had been at the centre of it.

The man himself died in a hotel room in New York in 1953. His last evening seems to have been wild. He visited at least eight bars and had numerous drinks in each; he was bodily removed from the fancy birthday party of a Manhattan socialite; before he took a cab to Harlem to score cocaine. Directly before he died, he was in the company of two young sailors, having had intercourse with both. They were asleep on the bed beside him when he pulled the trigger. It was, on the face of it, an extravagant case of suicide. Someone going out in the biggest way possible. But even people who weren't in the habit of giving credence to conspiracy theories, rarely believed it was so simple.

Also in New York that night was a former private detective who had turned bodyguard for Ravens. A man who disappeared into shadows at the death of his employer. While four blocks away, although the two had allegedly not seen each other in over a month, was his young wife, Emilia. The same woman who lay on a sun lounger in front of us now. It was seventy years after her husband's demise, and yet she appeared utterly fresh and desirable.

Her eyes were wide and chocolate brown, sparkling as she gazed at us with little more than cool detachment. Her nose was pert and pretty, but had a little kink at the bridge – a barely noticeable imperfection which increased her attractiveness. The lips she pursed at us were deliciously plump and no doubt prone to pouting. Her cheekbones were high and her jaw slightly pointed, but the smoothness of her skin removed any hint of the angular. You didn't look at her and see sternness, despite sternness being barely concealed below the beautiful features.

She hailed from the English Midlands, though her accent was cut-glass enough to be the product of the finest boarding schools. But her skin tone was olive, and her hair a luscious dark brown, so she could easily have been mistaken for an Italian beauty. She was a Claudia Cardinale who had never aged beyond her Sixties heyday. But a Claudia Cardinale who was never going to be able to pull off a winning smile. As every action from this woman came with obvious calculation.

She rose languidly into a sitting position and stared at us. A smirk, both amused and disdainful, crossed her lips. Then she swung her long, smooth legs round and planted bare her feet onto the floor. She winced a little as she touched the marble beneath her soles, although there was no way it could be hot yet. She was slim, yet almost unfeasibly busty. The swimsuit she wore was low cut, and another woman would have tried to cover herself quickly. This lady did reach for a short white robe at the end of the sun lounger, but the motion was without hurry. She gave the impression she had been interrupted from a wonderful dream and was intent on displaying her irritation at the fact.

Of course, Emilia Ravens had a file at The Organisation too. But despite the efforts of our researchers, we had never been able to find a birthdate or a correct place of birth. Both Nottingham and Derby had been suggested, but each could be wrong. The assumption was that, at some point early in her life, she had changed her name, adopted a whole other identity, and this was the reason for the murkiness.

It made sense. Jacob Ravens did not seem the kind of man who would be attracted to someone who was straightforward.

There had been various sketchy reports of her activities through the seven decades since her first husband's death.

Enough to more than convince us that she was still alive.

In late 1960, an Italian aristocrat encountered her in Sarajevo. He had romanced her before she married Ravens, but was now an elder gentleman with a cane. She made his day and stirred a thousand memories by sitting briefly once more on his knee. To his dying breath, he couldn't get over her unchanged freshness.

In 1973, a journalist was sent to interview her in Athens.

There was a solid lead as to her current whereabouts. But the young man was never seen again.

Another former acquaintance bumped into her at a party in St Lucia in the Eighties. The two women had been rivals in beauty after the war. But this woman was there now as a chaperone for her granddaughter. There was understandable shock then when she found her young heir in an amorous clinch with her own one-time, but completely unchanged, rival.

The last report we had of her in The Organisation's files was attending a birthday party in the Hollywood Hills in 2007, for the retired horror star, Raymond De Ville.

In each of these cases, it was the word of people who had known her before. Witnesses who understood the sheer impossibility of her being in the full flush of youth, but were convinced it was her, nonetheless.

And Ludo and I had the same thoughts. We had only ever seen her in photographs, but could recognise her instantly. This was Emilia Ravens and with her came a phenomenal beauty and a great darkness.

"Would you care for a morning *café au lait*?" she asked. "I'm personally of the opinion that coffee has enough flavour without adding milk, but I understand the modern trend is milk and lots of it."

Neither of us immediately spoke.

She was unabashed. "You will obviously have seen the glass of wine I was enjoying earlier, but I'm afraid I finished that particular bottle. I'm quite happy to open another one, if it would be more to your pleasure."

"Please, Mrs Ravens," said Ludo. "You didn't bring us all the way here for a coffee morning. Or for a wine tasting."

Her expertly plucked left eyebrow raised, and she stretched her long and perfectly formed legs. As she leant forward, I couldn't help but notice her nipples poking through the material of her swimsuit. Not that she would have cared where our gazes fell. As well as her beauty, her utter dismissiveness was obvious, Emilia Ravens wouldn't have cared any more about us ogling her, than she would have about falling under the gaze of an old cat. She may have summoned us here today, but we were – in the end – inconsequential to her.

She bounced to her feet, then sashayed towards us.

"Of course I haven't asked for your company to show off the quality of my beverages," she said. "I've brought you here because I want you to utterly destroy my husband."

CHAPTER SIX

In the surprised silence which followed, she walked past us into the house. The scent of her jasmine perfume filled my nostrils. Without a glance in our direction, she made her way to one of the couches and curled herself into it, folding her legs beneath her.

We followed and she nodded for us to take the couch opposite.

"Won't destroying your husband be rather difficult?" I asked.

"If we were take the public record at face value," said Ludo, "then Garris is correct. We'd have to conclude that there's more than half a century and an entire continent between us and the place he died."

She flashed a grin. Devastatingly beautiful, but with more than a hint of condemnation. It seemed she was going to pretend to be nice to us, but wasn't going to do a particularly good job of hiding the fact she was pretending.

"Oh, people who are supposed to be dead turning out to not actually *be* dead is very much a Jacob Ravens trope," she said. "I was hoping you'd be more expert in his work. With your profession, that your minds would be truly open to the impossibilities existence is capable of throwing at us.

That you'd be alert to the kind of things Jacob Ravens was capable of *beyond the grave*."

"I've read some of his work," I offered.

Ludo hesitated, and then added, "I dabbled at an early age, but I can't say I'm a fan."

"Really?" she asked.

"Yes, I don't know if this will offend you or not, but I always found the Ravens prose style quite difficult to get on with. It doesn't draw me in. Actually, it seems to be doing all it can to throw me clear."

She gave a little shrug. "To be honest, I always found it quite execrable myself. And I had to explain the fact to the man who literally wrote it, rather than to the woman who once upon a time – a very long while ago – was married to him, and wants whatever is left of him dead. And let me tell you, if you ever wanted to wound Jacob, going for his vanity was where to aim."

"If I'm in the mood, I'll perchance buy myself a copy and try anew," said Ludo. "I wouldn't be able to get one in an airport bookshop though, would I? In fact, it will be the more esoteric paperback merchants these days." He grinned. "Here's a curious thing which has occurred to me. You don't see Jacob Ravens on sale in the big bookshops in the Twenty-First Century, do you? But you seem to be doing okay. This place must cost a lot, and you're able to keep a vampire on retainer. But I'm guessing his literary estate isn't worth that much?"

She smiled at him; this time it came with a certain grudging admiration. "There were other things in his legacy beyond the literary rights."

The obvious question to have asked there was "what?" but neither of us tossed it into the mix. Instead she threw back her hair and then pulled the hem of her robe a little further down the top of her thigh, not that it did much to cover her long tanned legs. She regarded each of us.

"When I say I want you to destroy my husband, I do not mean the literal man who shagged his way around Europe and America all those years ago. The one who betrayed me in innumerable ways. No, he did indeed die in New York decades ago. I myself identified the body. There are a number of things I remember from that rainy night. An overweight, but strangely handsome, coroner who smelled of peppermint and would have propositioned me if my lawyer hadn't been present. He seemed the type. Jacob was laid on the steel counter. Utterly naked, with a bullet hole in his temple. They had washed off the worst of the blood. I put my finger inside the hole to make sure it was real. Reached all the way into his brains. Or what was left of them. It was squelchy and hot." She leant forward. "Do you think that's a normal thing to do?"

We both gawped at her, unsure what answer we could give. Both of us half-hypnotised by her wondrous brown eyes.

"Anyway," she continued, relaxing. "His body was taken and buried in an unmarked grave in Monterey. He had a house there, and he loved the ocean. Does that surprise you? People can be surprised to hear Jacob Ravens loved the ocean. It seems too normal for him. As far as I can tell, the body – his actual body – is very much there in the Monterey grave. But what I didn't realise, because no one bothered to tell the grieving widow, was that there was another ceremony which took place six thousand miles away, and something else which was buried."

Ludo nodded once. "This is the churchyard in England, isn't it? The one in Little Buxberry?"

Her eyes widened at him, genuinely surprised. "Well done, you! Don't you get the gold star!"

There was surprise obvious on my face too, and he turned to address it. "Don't you remember, Garris, what Elspeth Carmine told us? There was a grave with Jacob Ravens's name inscribed upon it and, after a tragic incident involving a teenage girl and murder, something dug its way from underneath."

I remembered. The night on the close in Milton Keynes.

Carmine's mellifluous voice relating the tale into the darkness.

Emilia Ravens stood and marched to the kitchen, knowing our gazes would follow her and not caring when her robe fell open. She stretched into one of the high cabinets and brought down a huge wine glass. Slightly tinted blue, and surely large enough to hold the contents of an entire bottle. Then she bent low and retrieved a bottle of white to fill it. I could just about read the label. It was a Napa Valley *Sauvignon Blanc*. As she moved, the ruby necklace glimmered on her neck. She opened the wine with a shiny silver corkscrew and poured half its contents into the glass, before taking a swig straight from the neck.

"I have decided," she said. "If no one wants a coffee, then I need a proper drink if we're going to discuss this." She put the bottle on the counter. "Obviously I've finished the red, but red is a far more after-hours drink, isn't it? Would you take a splash of white?"

"No thank you," I said. "It's early."

"Is it?" she asked. "We've all been awake for hours, and so what it says on the clock doesn't mean much anymore, does it?"

"I suppose not," said Ludo. "But we're working."

"And you can't drink on the job, ay?" She cocked her eyebrow at him. "Sounds excruciating. I would have thought the only thing which would get you through your job would be booze and lots of it."

She took a large sip from the glass and made her way to the sofa, slower and as if moving to music we couldn't hear. When she reached the cushions, she dropped herself down without spilling a drop.

"Do you remember Elspeth Carmine, Mrs Ravens?" Ludo asked.

"I've had a number of husbands since the days I was Mrs Ravens." This time she took a whole gulp of wine. "But I suppose, since I intend to disappear after this chat, Mrs Ravens will do fine. No. I do not recall anyone with the name Elspeth Carmine."

"He said he met you once. With your husband. In Fitzrovia."

"Did he say we went to bed together? Me and him. Or even the three of us."

I think I saw a flush on Ludo's cheeks at the directness of the question. "No, he didn't."

"Disappointingly they often tell an amorous tale, even if it's not remotely true." She grinned. "Your friend must be a gentleman then. It's good to hear of one in this day and age." Her eyebrow raised. "He also sounds like he's very old."

"He's been keeping an eye on the Little Buxberry churchyard."

I shot him a glance. How could he know that? In response, there was the briefest of smirks.

"It took me a little while to learn of this second burial," she said. "And at first I couldn't quite believe it. What would he have to bury after all? But then I discovered he had managed to remove a fairly crucial part of himself."

"What do you mean?" I asked.

A sour expression tainted her face. "He killed himself in New York! Don't let those fools on the internet tell you otherwise. The gun was in his hand and *he* pulled the trigger. I suppose, given what a trickster Jacob was, he may have put some of those rumours into the ether before he committed the deed. Anyhow, he made arrangements before he went that not all of him would be there. He removed a part of himself and that's what was buried. At exactly the same time as nearly everyone who knew him was weeping crocodile tears on the West Coast, this part of him was being buried in dingy old England."

"What was it?"

Emilia Ravens sniffed. "I suppose you could say it was his soul."

The word sat with us for a moment. Experiments had been run for thousands of years by people seeking to isolate the soul. But none of them, as far as anyone could tell, had ever succeeded. She held both our gazes, as if daring us to contradict her. But in my and Ludo's partnership, we'd had to accept a lot of seemingly impossible things. This past night we'd been ferried by a vampire to meet a young woman who we knew had first been married over seventy years earlier. Sometimes *impossible* is a word which doesn't mean anything.

"And what would the process be for that?" asked Ludo. "Carmine thought it might have been his heart which was buried. That seems quite prosaic in comparison."

She shrugged. "As I said, I learned this afterwards. Years afterwards. It gave me a chill. I'd seen his body and poked my index finger into what was left of his brain, but even as I did, there remained a sense I would never be free of him." She toyed with her necklace. "Well, I suppose I could make myself completely free of him, but I don't want to. As for what the process is for capturing one's soul, my understanding is samples were taken from him. His blood, his brain remains, his spinal fluid. Plus his semen and bodily waste. They were put together in a couple of jars and buried in a grave. Along with, and this might be the most gruesome part, the body of a recently murdered child, and a recently murdered fox. Over time, the three of them grew together. They became one creature. A being of death, with the soul and mind of Jacob Ravens."

It felt like the temperature dropped a couple of notches, despite the air conditioning purring.

"It was his brother, wasn't it?" Ludo said. "He handled the second burial."

"I suppose so, technically, but it was Jacob's doing in the main. One last prank from him to all the loved ones who wished him dead. Although he did get that lecherous giant toad, Arthur Haberdash to speak at that funeral. A man who would happily have killed Jacob himself if he could have done, but also, paradoxically, would have done anything for him.

"True, it was Jacob's brother who made all the practical arrangements. However, Gerald Ravens was such an inconsequential little man. An accountant by nature, if not by actual trade. I offered to have sex with him on the night of his wedding, just to see what would happen, and he could never meet my gaze afterwards. He also handled the Monterey burial, and part of me wonders what the hell he put in there."

"I'm sure we could get the necessary permissions to take a look into the Monterey grave if you wanted us to," I said.

She scoffed and took another glug. "It's unmarked, so I'm not sure how we'd find it. Besides, we've already got one body of his running free, we don't want to invite the other one to slip away. I'm prepared to believe that what's in Monterey is the real him. Or what is left of the real him. After all, the one in England was the perfect incubator. The grave was empty, anyone who found out about it was assured of that fact. *The grave was empty!*" She accentuated every word. "Therefore no one was going to investigate it, and if the ground was disturbed and something dug itself up, no one would expect to find anything there, anyway. There's almost an element of cruel genius to it. That and the fact Ravens evidently left enough clues in his fiction, so somebody eventually poured blood into the grave to set into motion the final awakening."

She laughed. "I guess, with the circumstances, having a vampire as my emissary to bring you here was the perfect choice."

"This is quite the story," I said.

"And yet I know you believe me," she said. "I am *the* unimpeachable source when it comes to Jacob Ravens. I haven't gone to all this effort to have a private one-to-one with you because I am a poor hysterical woman prone to flights of fancy. This is real, and we all know it for a fact."

Ludo leant forward on his seat. It was with an apologetic moue of his lips and a wave of his hand, but when he came to rest at the edge of the cushion, his gaze was one of utter interrogation.

"But why did he do this?" he queried.

She grinned, full and beautiful. "It's a good question. And one I cannot hope to answer. Except to say, the finality of death was something Jacob always expressed himself as being utterly bored with. A thing we have in common. But as for why he took this path? When you find him, you should ask him."

"Okay then," Ludo went on, "let me attack today from a different angle – why are you telling us this? Why have you gone through all this effort to get to us here? What does it matter to you if a remnant of your late husband is out there? You are an incredibly beautiful woman who must turn heads in every room you enter, and yet you are also a myth. A legend. No one is able to track you down unless you want to be tracked down. Not even Jacob Ravens, I imagine. So what do you fear from this man?"

"Thank you for the compliment." She sniffed. "You're right, I have been told I'm beautiful on many, many occasions, but never quite in such a fashion."

"Why do you want us to destroy your husband, Mrs Ravens?"

"Because…" She pondered for a few seconds. "I liked Jacob Ravens the best when I thought he was dead. When he was alive, he was never a good husband. To be fair, I was hardly a good wife. In death, well, he hasn't been bad." She waved her hand around at the luxury of the abode. "This thing which has emerged seems particularly dangerous, however. It's a few steps removed, and so I'm not sure it's completely my husband. I understand, for instance, that it might not answer to Jacob's name. Although I find it hard to believe it has lost all its conceitedness. Inevitably, it will have my husband's darkness and his hard-won knowledge. But it is a creature not of this world. One which owes its existence to murder and blood and strange magic. As such, whatever it is up to, it's better that it isn't allowed to get on with it."

"You're scared of it?"

It took her about ten seconds to reply. "I don't fear it will come for me. Instead I fear it will come for *everybody*." She sat forward, intensely meeting his gaze. "I know all about your Organisation, and what you do, and I understand this is your sphere of expertise. Investigating the possible return of Jacob Ravens is what you're supposed to do. You are the good guys and this thing, whatever he is now, is the walking personification of darkness."

On cue, the air conditioning clicked off. The atmosphere changed – only for a few moments – but I became acutely aware of the nervous sweat under my shirt.

"And what will you do?" I asked, trying not to swallow.

"Ha! I've done my bit. We're here, aren't we? You've listened to my story, and the vampire is getting a payday to last the next couple of lifetimes. Except he won't make it last long. What happens next? In approximately five minutes a car will arrive. Imagine its driver as the brother of the man you met earlier. A faithful retainer. I will get in the car and leave. Don't worry, my bags are already packed. You can then make a call to be picked up yourselves, and then you can decide what to do next."

"Okay," said Ludo, relaxing in the sofa. "You intend to disappear."

"Quite."

"The last time we have a record of you in our files, it was the 2000s…"

"2007," I chipped in.

"Yes, 2007," said Ludo. "I'm guessing you've learned more about disappearing than either of us can imagine."

She smirked. "2007, ay? As recent as that? It almost sounds like I'm losing my touch."

"So, if you know so much about hiding, maybe you can provide us with a little help on finding. How on earth are we going to locate this creature who may or may not be Jacob Ravens? It is an enormous world, after all."

The wine glass went to her lips, but it was more for a

gentle sip than a heavy gulp this time.

"Have you ever heard of a man named Earl Henderson?"

Ludo thought for a second. "I think the name might have been mentioned to us."

"He's based in Botswana these days, but if you ever want to speak to an expert on strange creatures and how to catch them, then he is your man."

CHAPTER SEVEN

Eventually Minako Cohen came and got us. It took her almost six hours to get there, in which time, Ludo and I searched the empty house for clues both of us knew wouldn't be there. When she'd managed to do it, I don't know, but Emilia Ravens had even removed the record which had been playing when we arrived.

All that remained was an old-fashioned stacked stereo from the 1980s.

Minako was The Organisation's representative on the West Coast of America. She had a small team she could assign to investigations, but a lot of her time was taken up liaising with the FBI and other interested agencies. If there was a real Mulder and Scully, then Minako would have their personal phone numbers. She'd lived in California for a couple of years, but was London by birth and upbringing, and seemed determined not to lose one shred of her accent, or the attitude which came from being a North London girl.

Of course we saw her approaching. By the point of her arrival, we had been staring bored at the desert for a good forty-five minutes. Her ride was a gleaming, red, convertible Chevrolet, and it was the perfect car for her. There's no way she could have driven it the whole distance from her home in San Francisco in this time, so she must have picked it up when she flew in. I wondered if she was ever going to return it. When she jumped from the car (not bothering to open the driver's door), she was wearing a blue and white floral mini-dress and knee-high grey suede boots, which added a couple of inches to her height. It was the kind of the outfit which would have been equally at home in a party or a pottery workshop.

"Wotcha!" she said. "You blokes in trouble again, are you?"

We'd greeted her downstairs, like the old friends we were, and filled her in on all that had transpired since we'd met Yardsmith in the long-ago casino. Minako was determined, now she was here, to take a gander at the house. "I'm unlikely to return this way anytime soon," she told us, as if this desert hideaway was merely a suburb she rarely visited.

"Sounds like you had a memorably glamorous encounter," she said, trotting eagerly ahead of us, while we pulled ourselves wearily back up the external staircase. "I can bring in a member of the team to dust for fingerprints, but – from what you say – I doubt we're going to find much."

"And we don't have her fingerprints on record anyway," I said. "So there's nothing to compare them with."

We made our way into the living area, and Minako exhibited great joy in rummaging through the kitchen.

"I wonder where she could have gone," she said. "Is it worth seeing if any of the private airports nearby had planes leaving today?"

"Perhaps," said Ludo as he dropped onto the sofa. "Although with the number of high-rollers who still frequent Vegas, they almost certainly will. We can also, I suppose, check the trains, and run facial IDs on passengers of every car. I suspect we don't need to check the greyhound buses. But then, she almost certainly knows we'd think that, so we should call her bluff and do it. Let's face reality, she's been practicing hiding herself since before any of us were born. If she wants to find us, then she'll find us. As was demonstrated tonight. While if we want to find her, it could take thousands of hours and we'd still get nowhere."

"Ludo's right," I said. I'd taken the other sofa, but I sat more forward and alert than he did. "We'll write it up in the file, and I'll put an alert out for agents to raise the flag immediately if they hear anything. But I'd be surprised if we get more than a whisper."

"Suit yourself," she said. "Personally I enjoy a challenge, but I also want to win at said challenge, so perhaps you're right."

Minako had found the stash of wine and retrieved three bottles of white and two of red. All of them from top Napa Valley vineyards – at least according to Minako. "If Mrs Ravens isn't going to return here, and at some point the air conditioning truly gives up the ghost, these vinos are all going to go to waste, aren't they?"

Neither of us made any objection.

"Minako," Ludo said, "did you get the chance, after we spoke, to look into this Earl Henderson character? I've heard stories about him, and I seem to remember one of the Australians mentioned him to us when we were occupied with the mirrors in Warsaw. I meant to have a further explore into what the man was up to when we got to London, but a lot happened that day."

A lot *had* happened that day. We'd found ourselves in a far-flung part of Siberia, trying to dodge the FSB, as well as a young woman who could suck the life from any man she met.

"We have a big, thick, juicy file on him," she said. "As you'd no doubt expect about anyone your new girlfriend mentioned to you, Ludo." She chuckled at her own joke.

Ludo maintained a fixed smile. As undeniably alluring as she was, the thought of actually being involved with Emilia Ravens raised more terror than lust.

"He's Irish American by birth," continued Minako. "But

he puts the emphasis very much on the former part. He was born in Kansas City, but his father was from Dingle, and apparently he has cultivated the brogue of someone from the far south-west of Ireland. He's seventy years old – birthday on Christmas Day – and is tall and imposing according to witnesses. Plays the country squire. Earl is his first name, but he treats it as his title. Everyone who deals with him is thus expected to use both names. He settled in Botswana ten years ago, buying himself hundreds of acres of land. Have you ever heard of Erskine Manor?"

We glanced at each other, and it was clear neither of us had.

"It's an exclusive reserve which Earl Henderson owns and runs. But not one you're going to buy entry into even through the most prestigious travel agents. You have to know someone who knows someone. Admittance is gained only by invitation. It's also devilishly expensive. A bauble of a treat those in the upper millionaire bracket have to save for. Billionaires probably wince when they have the cheques signed. When those people are not launching themselves on vanity missions into the upper atmosphere, this is the sort of place where they go and unwind. So it's a sealed-off reserve, geared towards those who tend to be close-lipped. But there have been rumours about it."

"What type of rumours?"

"He has a game reserve in Botswana," she said. "But rumours have always swirled that what's being hunted there is not your normal game. The authorities have investigated him more than once. But he has shown that the indigenous species are not only living, they're thriving on his estate. Which raises the question: if the stories of the hunts are true, what is being hunted?"

"The most dangerous game?" I ventured.

Minako crinkled her nose, pondering it. "Based on only the briefest skim of the information we have, I think it's going to be something different. That's the obvious thing to suspect, and after three investigations, you'd have thought evidence of man hunting man would have become apparent. Besides, they write books about that, they make films regarding it. I can't help feeling, whatever this is, it isn't going to be so easily guessable."

"Why haven't *we* investigated him before?" asked Ludo.

"Flicking through the digital file on the plane, which is all the information which has come our way, I pondered the same question. My only answer would be resources. Yes, there have been rumours, but if there has ever been anything more substantial, this Earl Henderson has been incredibly good at keeping it under his hat. It helps he's so public there, on various boards and committees. A loud voice in preserving the natural wildlife. But yes, there are a lot of stories, and for us it's best we finally take a look at them."

"So how do we get in there?" I asked.

"We have a man on the ground. Fusby is his name. I did part of his training, and he's very cute. He's met Earl Henderson, so that is a certain entrée."

"We go to his estate and try to join the hunt?"

"Oh, come on!" said Minako. "We can't afford the money which would be needed for such a gambit. That money is always earmarked for the higher-ups to buy themselves brandy. Nor do you two, if you don't mind me saying, have the prestige for them to roll out the red carpet for you."

I glanced at Ludo. After all the time we'd worked together, I didn't know too much about his family, but I'd gleaned that if they were not actually aristocratic, then they were aristocratic-adjacent. Minako's slight didn't seem to rumple him, however.

"I took the liberty of having a chat with HQ, and we think the best thing to do," she continued, "is to show your faces and say you're pursuing enquires. What enquiries and how much you tell him will of, course, be your choice. But say The Organisation's name, tell him you have jurisdiction in these matters and go from there."

"And if he doesn't want to be involved?" I asked.

She shrugged. "Then mention Emilia Ravens's name. She seems the sort of adolescent fantasy of a woman who people – *men* – want to hear more details about. I'm sure Earl Henderson will have heard of her. His curiosity will be piqued."

"Okay then." Ludo smiled. "It appears we are going to Botswana."

CHAPTER EIGHT

"Very pleased to meet you, gentlemen."

Our contact, Fusby, was younger than I'd imagined (although, yes, I could see why Minako had described him as cute). He sat, with his engine running, ready to pick us up at a private airfield thirty miles outside of Gaborone, and then ferried us away in a sleek air conditioned Range Rover. I couldn't help contrast it with the battered Volkswagen I was assigned in London, but then realised how terrible the suspension was on this Range Rover. It might have been shiny, but it wasn't the newest or best model. In the front passenger seat, I clung onto the handle by the door; while Ludo almost seemed to enjoy bouncing around the back.

Fusby was a tall, thin, but deceptively wiry guy, with a genuinely winning smile. Not only was he pleased to see us, but it might have been we were both already his best friends. He must have been in his late twenties or early thirties, yet could easily have passed as a teenager. He had smooth caramel skin, hair pulled into cornrows and wide sticking out ears, which – along with the gap-toothed smile he wore so prominently – gave him a goofy look. It was an appearance that, along with his youth, was going to lead to him being underestimated wherever he went. Something he was no doubt adept at exploiting. He had a sparkle in his eyes and walked with a skip. Making it all the more surprising when he gripped the steering wheel tight, changed gears with a fury and slalomed through the speeding traffic on the three-lane highway.

(To be fair, Minako was also a speed demon behind the wheel, and she'd exercised her need for speed when she took us to McCarran International Airport. But Fusby brought it to a whole new strata of recklessness.)

"Of course," he said, speaking loud enough to be heard above both the air conditioning and the stereo playing what sounded like K-Pop, "I worked for those creeps in MI6 first. Gopher work. Being their man on the ground, when their actual man on the ground found himself once more incapacitated by a hangover. On those many times he was out of action – or hiding from the husband of his latest piece of action – I was the one who'd step in and ensure any new arrival had everything they needed. I'd discover all the information I could to help them, and hope they mentioned my name in the dispatches to London."

"Sounds a promising arrangement," I said.

"It was until…"

He deliberately left the 'until' hanging. Almost winked as he invited me to ask the inevitable question:

"Until what?"

"Until the higher-ups discovered I had a certain amount of ESP. I can read other people's minds. Not a huge amount, and I have to physically touch them before I can get anything useful, but it was too much for those MI6 bods. It meant I couldn't be trusted with the wannabe James Bonds anymore. As I could easily put my hand onto their arm, in the spirit of friendliness, and hijack all the secrets from their minds. Or something. Those boys had signed the Official Secrets Act, and I hadn't, so that was that."

"Couldn't *you* have signed the Official Secrets Act?"

"I suggested that very course," he said. "It's what I said

to them. But the thing is with the Official Secrets Act, is all the secrets are on a need-to-know basis. They don't tell you *every* secret. That isn't the point of it. And since I had my ability, they'd have no way to check what I might become privy to. Which juicy little morsels I could prise from their agents' minds. No matter how inadvertent this prying might have been."

He spun us across three lanes of traffic and onto an exit ramp, seemingly without glancing in his mirror. Maybe as well as ESP, he had eyes in the back of his skull.

"It was all so ridiculous," he continued, "as the agents who are sent here are hardly the best. They're not the cream, more the condensed milk. Most of them, anyone with half a brain would have been able to read their secrets. You didn't need to have any extra special talent to know what they were or how they saw themselves. They might as well have arrived with Ray-Bans emblazoned with the words: *Ultra-Cool Spy Types*. So when they said I was a danger to them, it was absurd. I wasn't a danger to anybody. I was on their side. I could have helped them, if they'd directed me to shake hands with the right target. But they decided I was more dangerous than a man who got drunk and left a top secret file in a middle-aged prostitute's boudoir. Something which really happened, and which I – the man they threw out – spent thirty-six hours of his life successfully locating."

We both nodded sympathetically, and the effect seemed to make Fusby calm in his driving for a few seconds, before he decided to hit the accelerator and overtake a taxi at a corner. The beep from the irate cabbie echoed in our ears.

"Fortunately, word got to your organisation and they decided a man such as me, with good local knowledge, could be useful to them. It's a much more forward thinking body, and of course the ESP is a positive boon to them. Plus, I have now signed more than one Official Secrets Act."

"I'm going to guess you have shaken Earl Henderson's hand?" said Ludo.

"Oh yes, I've shaken the big man's hand. He clutches

tight when he does. He squeezes. I don't think he's aware of my talents, but if he did know, I don't imagine it would stop him. He would see my abilities as a challenge. His image is what he is. A big, jocular gent, with cold eyes and a razor's edge of danger. That's how he sees himself and that's how he sells himself."

"He sounds intimidating," I said.

He thought on it for a second and then swung off onto a battered, one-track road. Not that Fusby let such a detail influence his driving. If anything, he picked up speed.

"Yes and no," he said finally. "His size is large, and he likes to be the biggest man in any room, but when you meet him, he is charm itself. His voice is a rattling purr, even when he's saying things he wants to disturb your equilibrium. For instance, he knew I now worked for The Organisation."

"Did he?" I asked. "How?"

"I genuinely cannot say. I told no one but my wife. Of course I have to meet people like you when you come to the country, so undoubtedly he was able to put a couple of things together. But how he could learn who people such as you are, I can't fathom."

Ludo was clutching on to the back of both seats and pulling himself forward. "What did he say exactly?"

"It was the first time we met and we were shaking hands, and he said to me he knew I'd recently moved jobs and that he hoped I'd be happy in my new place, as it was a good *organisation*. He put the full amount of emphasis on the word, so I knew what he was talking about."

"And when he shook your hand, what did you get?"

"Power," he said. "And a need to be liked. This is a man who wants to be loved. Adored. But he also wants to terrify. Are there secrets in his soul? Of course there are. Yet none I could easily read. Really," he said, blushing, "he is the rare individual who I got no more from with my talent, than I would have done from astutely reading his body language. He is an open book, but also an utterly closed one."

"So what's your relationship with him today?" I asked.

"Oh, it's good," he said. "He's a man who wants to keep everyone on side. To give a show of the avuncular. So on the two times I've met him since, he's made a fuss, treated me like we're best friends. It's made what we're doing today a bit easier."

"What do you mean?"

"After talking with Minako, I called him to say I had two colleagues in town who'd be interested in meeting him. That you had a couple of questions for him. Not strictly protocol, I realise, but we thought it was the most prudent course. I didn't tell him you were from The Organisation, but he'll have surmised you are from The Organisation."

"And what's the upshot?" asked Ludo.

Fusby grinned at Ludo. Looking behind him and nowhere at the road. "You more than have your feet in the front door," he said. "Any friend of mine is a friend of Earl Henderson's and so on. I was going to take you to the apartment we rent in Gaborone tonight, but I am driving you straight to him. For better or worse, you are Earl Henderson's guests tonight."

CHAPTER NINE

Three large white men with Kalashnikovs, muscles and scars stood as sentries at the high barbed-wire topped gates of Earl Henderson's estate. They didn't smile as we drove up. Behind their sunglasses, they didn't offer any welcome at all. I wondered whether that would be the case if we'd arrived by limousine, but then decided I couldn't imagine any of them smiling. They were an impressive show of force, rather than a red carpet. A sense of security that the outside world was well and truly locked at a distance, thus adding to the air of exclusivity. They were supposed to scare away those with less than seven figures in their bank accounts. But, ostentatiously undaunted, Fusby skidded to a halt next to them and revealed his never-ending, ingratiating smile.

"You okay there, Lennie?" he called.

I don't know which one was Lennie. None of them responded, none of them did more than glance in his direction.

"I hope the Missus is feeling better now," he persisted.

As promised, we were expected. They might have ignored Fusby's chatter, but one of the men nodded towards a tucked away colleague the other side of the gate, and the heavy metal barrier slid open before us.

Then once more, we were driving through acres of unspoiled desert, only on Earl Henderson's high-fenced, private game reserve. And because there was nothing on the roads, Fusby determined to really see what the Range Rover could do. His foot went full on the accelerator and he sported his most gigantic grin yet.

Ludo stayed on the edge of the back seat, clinging onto our seats.

"Are you sure such speed is wise?" I asked.

The grin finding space to grow wider, Fusby turned his head and stared at us both. Eyes off the road. "Do you doubt my abilities? Sure, I haven't done one of those fancy driving courses you're supposed to do in London, but the thing is, I reckon I could show you a thing or two."

"You could," acknowledged Ludo. Who, despite it being a prerequisite of our job, hadn't got around to the most basic driving course, let alone the more advanced one. "The thing is, however, isn't the point of this place that there are large mammals about? You don't necessarily have miles and miles of open road ahead of you. What if something were to step in front of the car?"

Fusby turned and looked at what was ahead, and his foot may have let up on the accelerator a little. Not enough to be safe, however.

"You'd think so, wouldn't you?"

"What do you mean?"

"Most hunts on these reserves take place in the day. Better visibility. Safer for the hunting party. But, allegedly, Earl Henderson always makes it a point to send his guests out at night, and no night vision goggles are allowed. He says the creatures he hunts only emerge in the night, so it's only sporting to hunt them on their terms."

"And we have no idea what they are hunting?" I asked.

"There's a corner of this estate sealed off for elephants and giraffes and the like. That's where the inspectors get taken when they come and visit." Fusby explained. "But men – and it's always men – come from all across the world to hunt here. Rich guys who arrive on private jets for the Earl Henderson experience. Whatever it might be. The fact they come repeatedly, means they are happy with what they hunt here. But what are they hunting? Surely if they have transported in the bigger nocturnal hunters from elsewhere in Africa, then they would need their own prey. We might not see them in the daylight, but we would see the creatures they themselves fed on. But there's very little, isn't there?"

"And no one is alarmed by this?" Ludo said.

"There are never any complaints. If any of these billionaires come away unhappy, they're tight-lipped. In the local government offices, those who rubber-stamp the licences have heard rumours and grasped there's something odd afoot, but so far have been satisfied by Earl Henderson's sanitised tour. I've sent reports to The Organisation, and received responses asking questions, but I can't – on the ground – give them anything more than gossip."

"And what gossip is that?"

"Vampires. Werewolves."

I did my best not to shudder at the second word.

Was it my imagination, or did Fusby shoot me a glance from the corner of his eye?

He continued. "When you say to someone there are predators here which no one outside ever sees, and which rich men pay a lot of money to hunt, then their minds are only going to go in only a couple of directions."

"Most vampires fly under the radar," I said. Thinking of Yardsmith and how grateful he was for his money.

"And not as many werewolves lose control as is commonly supposed," Ludo said, with a reassuring pat on my shoulder.

"I know." Fusby said. "The thing is, most people don't appreciate these nuances. If there's an animal truly secret being hunted here and it only comes out at night, what is it, if it's not those two things?"

We drove on in silence. Not merely in the car, but all around us. The surroundings, as they whizzed past, appeared beautiful, but empty. There was nothing there. The wide spaces meant, at the speed we were travelling, I could determine passing details. But I didn't spot any birds in the sky, nor larger creatures moving in the distance. All was desolate, so we could have been driving on a moonscape which had grown shrubs.

Eventually, in the far distance, a house appeared. The building had to be five miles away when I first noticed it, but already it was making its presence known. It was not at all what one would expect from this African landscape, and yet seemed to fit in with all I'd heard of the man who lived there. An edifice of grey brick rising from the red soil. A baronial manor house. It reminded me of Killamurray Castle, which we'd visited for a matter in Ireland a little while ago – although this was far more imposing. It was gothic and sprawling and dominated the surrounding landscape.

We watched it grow bigger and bigger. Every couple of hundred yards, it seemed to swell to a more impressive size. We could see the turrets at each side and get an impression of just how far back the building extended. At the centre of its frontage was a tall, wide arch, which really should have had a portcullis ready to drop down. As far as I could see, there was no moat or drawbridge. But I couldn't help thinking, both would have been discussed at the design stage.

The nearer we got, the more Fusby watched his speed. A respectful gesture. It wouldn't do to arrive at Earl Henderson's actual home in a recklessly driven vehicle.

There was an individual already waiting for us in front of the house. It seemed to me we could see this man – and it was only one man – a couple of miles ahead as well. He was tall and broad and solid-looking. As sturdy as the house itself. His hair was silver, and he had a lined and grizzled face. Suggesting several lifetime's worth of experience.

There were puffy, heavy bags under his eyes, but they were a sign of character more than tiredness. And to add the impression we had been transplanted to another time and in another country, he was wearing a red hunting jacket and spotless white jodhpurs.

The closer we got, the more the eyes were drawn to him, rather than to the house behind him.

He had a grin on his wide face and his hand outstretched before Fusby pulled the handbrake.

"Mr Garris and Mr Carstairs. I am Earl Henderson. I have heard of your reputations. Much the same as you, I'm sure, have heard of mine. It is a pleasure to welcome you to my abode. To my *Palace of Play*."

CHAPTER TEN

Inside it was harder to conceive that we were within driving distance of Gaborone. Earl Henderson had furnished the main living area as if it was his boyhood dream to live in a Galway hunting lodge. An old stone fireplace dominated the room. A blaze roaring within it. It was hot outside, but such a detail wasn't going to dissuade a man like Earl Henderson. (I could only imagine the air conditioning was turned high to compensate.) Around the walls were oak panelling and mounted hunting trophies. Both bear heads and lion heads. The type of souvenirs which were either ridiculously old or squirmingly illegal. There were hunting rifles affixed to the wall, each undoubtedly with a story to tell. Furthermore, there were two impressively heavy bookcases. I didn't venture close to them, but Earl Henderson did not appear the class of man who would have a lot of frivolous paperback fiction. I spotted an aged edition of *The Collected Tales of Sherlock Holmes*, as it was so prominent. Beyond that, it seemed to be hunting volumes and tales of true-life daring. So-called men's books.

In front of the fire were arrayed expensive and comfortable leather chairs. Their arms worn by use. There were tables between them, loaded with boxes of cigars and decanters of whiskey and cognac. It was a room for the wealthy and the influential. But a place they could convince themselves they were slumming. There wasn't even mobile phone service. I was from a lower middle class background near Bristol. Really, the only reason I should have been invited into this room was to serve the drinks. Not long ago we had met Manuel Pompidou, the former head of declining social media network, Amigo. This was the kind of place he would have visited. He and his peers in the uber-rich, sitting together and telling themselves how clubbable they were, while comparing piles of bank notes.

The chair nearest the fire was more of a throne. It was taller and wider than all the others, and the cushions were extra thick. It wouldn't have been a shock to learn that it was Henry the Eighth's own personal armchair. The one he'd sat in, through the long winter evenings at Hampton Court Palace, expensively imported along with everything else. It didn't surprise me at all when Earl Henderson claimed it. Of course it was his. And the private table of dark alcohol and cigars besides it was his to consume on his own. He sat carefully, almost gingerly – compared to the vigour of the rest of his movements – then he positioned himself as a king. Which he was. The men who came here, the ones he entertained, may have been richer and more influential than he, but this was *his* domain.

He waved his hand beneficently and signalled for the three of us to sit as well. We each chose a chair. They were firm and supportive. A sedentary man with a dodgy back, who'd spent all night traipsing around the bush, would appreciate the comfort.

"Well then," said Earl Henderson, beaming his crooked grin at us. Much more munificent and grander than Ludo's grin. "The first thing is always the first thing. Can I provide you gentlemen with a beverage?"

"I'll have a water please," I said.

"Me too!" echoed Ludo.

"*Water?*" Earl Henderson barked at us aghast. This was obviously the most unreasonable of unreasonable demands. "Have you arrived in my company already appallingly drunk?"

"Um, no," said Ludo. It was rare to see Ludo Carstairs baffled, but this was one such occasion.

"As the only possible use for water is to steady one's legs after you have been drinking alcohol for a good twenty-four hours plus." Earl Henderson stated. "The best of us might find the world become a tad shaky beneath our feet after such an endurance test. Then, if the man does not want to waste his time with sleeping, water becomes a respectable choice. Just to ease the pressure on the kidneys and liver and make sure all those boring innards, which hide away as they know they are so boring and irritating, keep you fresh and standing. Once you have consumed the water..." He interrupted himself. "No more than two glasses, mind you, you do not want to undo all your splendid efforts by taking too much water. Then you can move back to the proper stuff. But that is the only purpose for a glass of water."

Ludo smiled at him. "What would you suggest we drink then?"

Earl Henderson pondered, a certain disdain playing on his lips. "The closest thing I have to water is a cold lager beer. I do not enjoy the stuff myself. Neither the taste, nor the bubbles, particularly appeal to me. But I understand it has a following. Especially amongst younger men. But if you are feeling thirsty, then it is the beverage I would recommend. I will have Horatio bring a glass."

I hadn't noticed Horatio before, but he was standing in the doorway. A tall, spare white man with a bald head, who was utterly skeletal. He nodded once.

"I'll have a lager as well then, please," I said. We'd spent hours on aeroplanes and then had a drive in the heat (albeit in an air-conditioned car) and absolutely I could have done with water, but it wasn't a thing I could insist on.

Earl Henderson beamed. "And Mr Fusby will have a

port. We have already established that in our acquaintance. It is another drink I am not partial to, yet I admire it more. It has a certain kick to it. It says a man is not dancing around the edge of serious drinking, but is ready to commit to it. He is prepared to make the Herculean effort to get truly and properly drunk."

"Thank you," said Fusby, with a cheeriness which no one else in the room exhibited. "But before I met you, I was still drinking rum and colas."

Earl Henderson chuckled. "But you listened when I explained the ways of the world to you. There is more to being a man than the taste of conquest, and the desire for fornication. I would not say you were my best pupil, as it is not as if you have appeared for any more lessons. You have a great deal to learn regarding the business of manliness. But in the brief time we had together, you were without a doubt one of my most receptive pupils." He peered to the doorway. "Come along, Horatio! You are not paid to lollygagger."

With another nod of the head, the man disappeared.

Earl Henderson narrowed his gaze against Ludo. "If we are able to spend significant time together, Mr Carstairs, then I would take the opportunity to educate you."

"Educate me?"

"Yes, I imagine you have arrived today and asked for water because you consider yourself thirsty. But you do not drink water to quench a thirst. For that, you use alcohol. Always alcohol. Sink it down, a little something to bite the thirst. You use alcohol to beat the thirst, then when the thirst has submitted, you decide whether you want to use alcohol to get drunk. And if you make that decision, then you get drunk seriously and without remorse. You must never, ever use anything as pathetic as beer to get yourself drunk. Not if you are a man. The same goes for wine. Port wine I will obviously make an exception for. As a starter, anyway. No, when you want to get drunk, you reach for the serious stuff. You make it both your friend and your enemy.

A passion to put your arm around and hold, but also know you want to force it to the ground and prove you are indeed the strongest. That is the way you drink, Mr Carstairs. Mr Garris, too." He waved a little finger in our direction. It was so big, it seemed he'd be able to win arm wrestling bouts with it, "Try not to forget this useful information."

"I'll try," said Ludo, seeming more amused than annoyed.

"I cannot blame you, I suppose, both your accent and your name are obvious clues of your providence. London is not a drinking town. I am well aware it likes to pride itself as such, but it is full of amateurs playing a serious game and not doing it properly. Any night you promenade the streets, you will find men and women who have got drunk in entirely the wrong fashion. People who have not understood the concept of it at all."

"I live in Copenhagen."

"Ha!" he half laughed and half cheered. "Now *there* is a drinking town! Copenhagen is a place which does it properly. I am not sure the Danes have worked out yet how to take joy from their drinking. That is their flaw. But this is an echo from their Viking past. They need to be watchful while in their cups. But they are a people who slowly and steadily imbibe with a seriousness I can admire."

Horatio came with the drinks. I was somehow expecting our lagers to be served in giant tankards, which Earl Henderson would try to make us down in one. But fortunately they arrived in neat little half-pint glasses, thick and not easily broken, and with a pleasing chill to the touch. I wondered how many of the tycoons and the captains of industry who came here had heard similar speeches.

Earl Henderson was handed a glass far bigger than ours. His was brimming with whiskey.

"Well then, gentlemen," he said, after taking a healthy gulp. "You have come a long way. What can I do for you?"

I shifted forward in my seat. Given the height and bulk of both Earl Henderson and his chair, he was always going to loom over us. I did what I could to change the balance. For me to meet him as an equal. Even though I knew it wasn't go to work. "We'd like to talk to you, if we can. To ask you some questions about Jacob Ravens."

He chuckled to himself.

"I take it you've heard the name?" said Ludo.

"I have heard a great many things in my life and one of those is, yes, the name of Jacob Ravens."

"What have you heard of it?"

He took another big gulp of whiskey. "Oh, I am an old man. And we old people have a habit of pretending we have seen everything before. With all the changes in technology the modern world has wrought, we still convince ourselves we have seen versions of it all in our younger days. It is a way to make things seem more comforting. Or to be outraged by the way things have transpired. As they did not happen that fashion in the bygone more civilised times. The life I have led, of course, means I am less surprised than most. I have seen so, so, so much." His gaze moving dreamily into nothing. "But I will happily concede that Mister Jacob Ravens has surprised me."

Ludo kept his own gaze fixed unerringly on Earl Henderson. "What do you mean?"

Our host took a last big gulp, slipping back most of the contents of the glass. Then he signalled to us to do the same. Ludo and I did, although neither of us got close to consuming the whole glass. The bubbles hit my throat and nearly brought up an unfortunate belch. Only Fusby stayed his wrist, and – annoyingly – Earl Henderson seemed to appreciate him for not being bullied. Giving him a nod of approval.

"What do I mean?" Earl Henderson ruminated. "I don't rightly know how to answer the question. Yes, I have been shocked by a few of the stories I have heard, but they largely exist within the realms of rumour and conjecture." He beamed his big crooked grin at us. "And, gentlemen, do I look like a gossiping washer-woman to you?"

"Of course not," said Ludo.

"And with all the things which are said about me, which mostly only have a sliver of a connection to reality, I am not one to hand credence to scuttlebutt and hokum."

"They've come a long way, Earl Henderson," said Fusby, finally taking a sip of his large glass of port. "We understand what you're saying, but it'd surely be wrong to send us off again completely empty-handed."

Earl Henderson nodded once. "You are right, my friend, of course you are. I can either pride myself on being an excellent host, or I cannot. And I always do." His rumble of a chuckle came. "I will tell you the facts in my possession, gentlemen. But first Horatio will fetch me another drink. I have a feeling it is going to be a long night."

CHAPTER ELEVEN

"Despite these wrinkles on my face and the bags under my eyes, I am not old enough to have met the man himself," Earl Henderson said, with a fresh glass of whiskey swilling in his large hand. "I am not as old as I look and I am not as old as I feel, but that is a whole other story. I am most definitely aware of Jacob Ravens's presence. Most certainly I am."

"Are you a fan?" asked Ludo. "I don't mean to cause offense, but his books don't seem the type that would appeal to you." He waved his hand in the direction of the ultra-masculine volumes on the shelves.

Earl Henderson grinned, but this time it didn't reach his eyes. "Do you think we are far enough into our friendship for you safely to judge me, Mr Carstairs? For you to pack me neatly into boxes? You have seen that particular bookcase, but this is a large house, and you know nothing of the other bookcases." His teeth were large, and the many, many wrinkles on his face gave the grin a simian quality. "Nor can you say what currently lies on my bedside table."

Ludo nodded his apology.

"I remember you saying," said Fusby, leaning forward and trying to smooth things over, "that most of the items in this room were for show. The kind of objects a guest would imagine a room like this would contain."

"Your recollection is correct," said Earl Henderson. "Mr Carstairs, in his presumptuous way, is also correct. The works of Jacob Ravens have not appealed to me in the slightest. In fact, I have never read a word of his."

"They don't hold a great appeal to me either," said Ludo, doubtless now feeling himself on safer ground. "I've only dabbled."

"Really?" Earl Henderson's eyebrow arched. "That surprises me. I would have thought, a man in your profession, would be more of a connoisseur."

"There are so many things to read," I said. "So many better things."

"Yes," said Ludo. "Connoisseurs enjoy things of finer quality."

Earl Henderson gave a volcanic rumble of a chuckle. "They do! I appreciate men who read, gentlemen. I champion men who read and men who drink and men who are unafraid of the hunt. At the moment I am pegging you, in my own presumptuous way, as being only one of the three. But you are young, so I can train you. You too, Mr Garris. However, to return to the matter at hand, I have never read anything by the author, Ravens. But I have cultivated a strange fascination with him. Particularly, and I am going to guess this is the reason for your arrival on my doorstep, with regards to his afterlife."

None of us said anything in response.

He relaxed in his chair and drained half of his glass. If it was me who had consumed that much, I'd already be slurring my words, but it barely seemed to affect Earl Henderson.

"Well then, gentlemen, it seems to me I am the one expected to do all the work here. You have come to my property because you want information from me. You have come to me, as it were, to seduce me. To bring me around to your side. But, as it is transpiring so far, you seem to think you can sit there with a grubby five-dollar bill in your hand and get me to perform a striptease. Well, I am afraid it does not work in this fashion. I am a man with a certain level of class and you need to earn your prize."

Ludo and I glanced at each other. "What are you suggesting?"

"If you show me yours, then I'll show you mine." He beamed.

"You want us to tell you what we know?"

"Quite."

Fusby shifted again in his chair. "It's not like we don't trust you, Earl Henderson. It's just we've signed numerous pieces of paper telling us not to say things aloud."

He waved his hand dismissively through the air. "Do you think I have respect for your pieces of paper? Or what promises you have made to nameless states and shifty governments? Do you imagine I am going to call your starched shirt bosses afterwards and tell them what disgraceful blabbermouths you have been? Of course not."

Fusby started to protest: "We don't think that…"

But Earl Henderson talked over him: "You have come here to ask me about a specific matter, and the only information I require also relates to that matter. Wider secrets be damned! I have no room for them in my ears today! But if you want me to tell you what I have gleaned concerning Jacob Ravens and his strange afterlife, then you are going to have to tell me what *you* understand about Jacob Ravens and his strange afterlife."

Ludo didn't hesitate any longer. "We know there was a grave bearing his name in the English countryside. Although his actual body was buried thousands of miles away. Two young people were found dead on top of this grave. And, if the stories are to be believed, that same night something climbed out from under the soil. What it actually was, we can't say. But whatever it was, it allegedly contains the essence of Jacob Ravens. His soul. His knowledge as well. Whatever it is, wherever it is, it seems like it would be a good idea for us to have a conversation with it."

Our host nodded three times in quick succession. He had listened intently to Ludo's precis, but there was no shock on his features. "My personal understanding is they buried a dog and a couple of cats. Not any dog, a big old Alsatian which was wild in its nature and whose owner found impossible to get under control. It was the closest thing they could get to a wolf in England at that point."

"We heard it was a fox," I said.

"A fox?"

"Yes." I swallowed. "It was Jacob Ravens's bodily fluids. A recently slain fox, and the body of a recently murdered child."

For the first time, we appeared to have shocked him. He stared still and straight ahead for a good thirty seconds.

When he then spoke, it was in a low hushed tone. "As distressing as it is to consider, I can believe the story of the child. This is the people they were, after all. As for the fox…" He shook his head. "No. A fox is vermin, and anyone trying an experiment such as this, would automatically gravitate to an animal more regal.

"I heard they slit the dog's throat the same night the word reached them from New York that the man himself was dead. The cats' too. They were feral toms. The process needed creatures who would accept the essence of the man, and so it wasn't the case they could use rabbits or hamsters."

"Where did you hear your information?" Ludo asked.

He shrugged and laughed. "How did I know they had two pints of Jacob Ravens's blood already congealed in jars before this experiment? Who told me about the spells uttered over the graveside by a man named Haberdash? A former mentor to Ravens, who performed his incantations under the pale moonlight? How do I know that those who interred the body reached the end of their lives thinking themselves failures as the great Ravens had not returned?"

"Yes," said Ludo. "Where did you hear all of that?"

His gaze brushed across all three of us.

"I am aware of these facts because I am a man who has met a lot of people with an interest in the peculiar and esoteric, and has thus heard a great many hair-raising tales. These stories have been related to me across decades, from different corners of the world. However, they have been on my mind recently. I have been collating them. And I have been performing this exercise because the creature which finally raised itself from the dirt that night has made contact with me."

We stared at the big man, who pursed his lips in appreciation of our reaction.

I put my glass to the table, not wanting to spill a drop. "Why did the creature make contact with you?"

"For the simple reason, Mr Garris, that I am a man who intuits how to find things. Much the same as yourselves, the strange is my business. My bread and butter, as you English say. I merely approach it from a different angle to you. The creature which emerged from the grave was lucky. The man Ravens and his acolytes did not think it would take so long for somebody to interpret the clues he had left. It was going to take five years for the various body parts to merge themselves together, but after that, everything was in place for the resurrection. But no one did what they were supposed to do."

"Ravens's work had fallen from fashion," I said.

He nodded. "However, if this creature *had* emerged in, say, 1960 – there would not have been an Earl Henderson to help it. I was six years old then, and in no fit state to do dealings with creatures from far beyond the veil. But, the item this new creature which was born of Ravens wanted, I was able to find and deliver to him. Do you know what I call it, by the way?"

"We heard it doesn't answer to Jacob Ravens."

"I call the entity in question The Ravens Creature. It sees distance between itself and the man. Perhaps it has determined itself to be a superior version. Anyhow, I made a successful delivery to The Ravens Creature. We had a satisfactory transaction. And I am sure if it requested something else, we would repeat the process. I have no qualms about who or what I deal with, life is too short to let a conscience weigh heavily."

"What did you sell him?" Ludo asked.

"No," Earl Henderson said, firmly. "I do not think I want to get into that. Instead I have a question for you. As I cannot imagine it is the chatty sort, what connected it to me in your minds?"

"Emilia Ravens suggested we should talk to you," said Ludo.

His entire face lit up. Obviously Minako's feeling that the woman would intrigue him was correct.

"Ah, Emilia. The lovely, wondrous, beautiful, utterly dangerous Emilia. I do not mean to brag out of class, however in the occasional instance it is almost impossible not to do so. I once had a night of passion with Emilia Ravens. Her body entwined with mine. It was at the Chateau Marmont, and it transpired it was the same night as the comedian John Belushi died. Do you know of him? I never found him amusing myself." He sniffed. "When we saw the sirens, we thought the intensity of our lovemaking might have started a fire."

He chuckled silently to himself and finished off the second glass. Without him glancing, Horatio was at his side ready to take it for a refill. He hadn't offered us a further round of drinks, but maybe there was a house rule that guests could have what they wanted of any beverage, apart from water or lager.

There were those decanters on the table, after all. If we were feeling manly enough.

"Can you tell us where this creature is?" I asked.

He held his freshly delivered glass to his lips, but didn't take so much as a sip from it. His gaze scanned the three of us.

"I am a fair man," he said. "Would you say you are fair men?"

"I would think so," said Ludo.

"Absolutely!" said Fusby.

"Good," Earl Henderson purred, before fixing on Fusby. "I am sorry, old friend, as I am going to make it seem I am excluding you. And that is not my intention. But, in another way, I suppose it is. You appreciate I have the highest of regards for you. I believe there are few finer men anywhere else in this blessed country. But I want to make a deal with your companions here."

"We all work together," Fusby said. "Whatever you say to them, you can say to me."

"The *saying* is not the issue," Earl Henderson told him. "I am not going to let loose such information while receiving nothing in return. I may be generous, but I am not a sucker. There is something I will want these two men to do for me before I hand over the information I have, although it comes with a certain level of danger."

"What type of danger?" Fusby queried.

"Life-threatening," said Earl Henderson baldly. "Well, it would be life-threatening for a man who was not too bright and not too capable, but both these men strike me as having more than adequate supplies of both. So they should be fine. However, it is there and if anything goes wrong this dark night, I want you to tell the world I played fairly. I want you to swear that you will do so, Mr Fusby. If all three of you drive onto my land and do not return, then I am inviting all kinds of trouble onto myself. Yet, if you are able to emerge the other side and swear I played fairly with your colleagues. That any misfortune which occurred was just bad luck on Mr Carstairs's or Mr Garris's part, then you will be listened to. Do you swear to do that?"

Fusby, who had been nursing his glass, placed it firmly on the table. "If I don't?"

The big man shrugged. "Then we shall all move on with our lives. I will bid you good day and we can all return to our peaceful, or not so peaceful, existences. Not as friends as such, but as slightly more than acquaintances. It is a fact, however, that I have information you need, and this is the only way you are getting it."

"He'll do it," said Ludo. "He'll swear."

"Will I?" asked Fusby.

"Yes, you will. It will be alright."

I wished I felt as confident as Ludo did.

"Good," said Earl Henderson. "Excellent news. What I would like you to do, gentlemen, is to spend a night on my grounds. All my guests spend the night on the grounds; it is part of my conditions for coming here. Once you have done what I ask, once you have spent the night outside, you can walk in here tomorrow morning at breakfast and I will provide you with a hearty feast and all the information you seek."

"Do you have men with rifles who'll hunt us?" I asked.

He laughed. "Mr Garris, unlike Mr Carstairs, I see you read your share of sensationalist literature. No, I would never do something so passé. There is danger there, of course there is. What would be the point of doing it unless you had your adrenalin pumping? But you will have every chance of keeping yourselves safe. In fact, I have all the confidence in the world that you will return with a sense of achievement and a story to tell. Then I will shake you both by the hands and impart my knowledge to you. What do you say?"

I turned towards the window, knowing I wouldn't be able to see anything beyond the slowly setting sun. "What's out there?"

"Possibly nothing," he said, sounding both Irish and charming. "I am sure that men like you have stayed in the odd old house which is supposed to be haunted."

We glanced at each other. Killamurray hadn't been that long ago.

"And, despite psyching yourselves up for it, how often do ghosties actually appear?" he asked.

On that occasion they very much had, but the proper answer was a lot more mundane.

"Rarely," said Ludo.

"Quite. I have done this before with a good number of individuals. A good proportion of whom have come in for breakfast wondering what on earth this old crank was playing at. Why I would feel the need to test them by letting them sleep in beautiful scenery under a vast starry sky. Others," he said, "have had a more adventurous time of it."

"Adventurous how?"

"It is for you to learn."

"But why?" asked Fusby. "And why not include me? I am as much of The Organisation as they are."

Earl Henderson stiffened a little in his giant chair, a parent getting ready to admonish his child. "I have already explained my reasons why. Should the worse happen, and I do not expect the worse to happen, then you are the witness as to my excellent character. Yes, you would have to tell your bosses about the deal which was made, but you would also explain how Mr Garris and Mr Carstairs were willing parties to it. They signed up. And…" He let the sentence trail off.

"And what?"

"They are Organisation men from London."

"What difference does it make?" Fusby, for the first time, sounded agitated.

"Because I was in London a very long time ago and I met a person who worked for The Organisation." He gave us his biggest and most self-satisfied smile. "He was more of a consultant than a worker by that point. This was 1969. I was a broad-shouldered teenager, and he was in his sixties. You may have heard of him. His name was Paul Raeker."

I resisted the urge to gasp. "You knew Paul Raeker?"

"He was one of your original agents, wasn't he? One of your founders. He worked for British intelligence in World War Two, he told me, and afterwards it was decided his skills were needed in this new body."

"How did you meet him?" asked Ludo.

Our host shrugged. "Let us say, we were hunting the

same quarry. I will tell you in greater detail one day. Maybe. But it might be something to do with the moon landing and the possible return of Spring-Heeled Jack. Exciting for a young man. Exhausting for an old man suffering the onset of emphysema. But a good story nonetheless. Suffice to say, it has made me always eager to test the mettle of Englishmen. Particularly Englishmen in your line of work."

"Hang on…" said Fusby.

But Earl Henderson raised his big hand to stop another word. "I admire you Mr Fusby, I do. I esteem you greatly. However, from this point on, your presence is not required. I would be grateful if you would leave the room please. If your colleagues make the decision that my deal is not worth taking, then I am sure they will leave in five minutes to tell you so. You can all drive away together. Nobody will stop you. But, should you not have heard from them in that period, then you are to climb into your vehicle and depart. Leave my property. Go to your office, or your pretty young wife, and wait for them to call. Which I am sure will happen at first light."

Fusby went to protest further, but he also half stood. Such was the power of Earl Henderson's voice and the force of his personality, it was hard not to follow his commands.

"It's okay," said Ludo. "We are taking up Earl Henderson's time and we want the information he has, so we will listen to what this entails. And if we decide to do it, we will do it to the best of our abilities and call you tomorrow."

"I commend your spirit!" cheered Earl Henderson. "I knew I'd like you."

Fusby was clearly unsure, but started towards the door. "I'll wait ten minutes. I know you said five, Earl Henderson, but I'll stay there for ten. Just in case."

"As you wish," said our host.

We all watched him depart in silence, then when the door had closed, Ludo asked: "What is this really about?"

"There is no ulterior motive beyond that which I have

stated. I want to test your mettle, to see what you are made of. I am old-fashioned and, I suppose you would say, I am of the ancient school. Too many of you modern men seem to lack gumption and spirit. At least, that is how it feels to my tastes. I want to make sure you are not amongst them. I want to know those with whom I work and those with whom I drink."

"And you want to test us against Paul Raeker?" I said.

"Yes, I do." The big man smiled. "You have asked me for the favour, have you not, Mr Garris? You are putting yourself in my debt. As such, I have to have a sense of who I am dealing with."

"We're already getting a sense of who *we're* dealing with," said Ludo.

"Good!" he boomed. "Well, it is time for you to step up. There is nothing of nature which is going to eat you out there. But there is a moon and plenty of stars. And at night, both cast incredibly long and dark shadows. It is a bleak wilderness, and can drive weaker men mad with fear from their own imaginations. I simply want to make sure you are not amongst them."

"And what can we take with us?" I asked. My gaze landing on the rifles on the walls.

"Normally, I have men discreetly watching. To make sure no real harm befalls. But that's a perk for the paying customers. For you, simply what you have with you should suffice. It is not too cold this time of year. I will, however, be fair to you." He reached into a carved teak box beside his chair and opened it. Inside were aligned eight silver flasks. They gleamed in the light and he held them for us to each take one. "What I would ask is to hold onto one of these. There is moisture in a desert at night. More moisture than people appreciate. But still, those who are inexperienced can become thirsty. And I would hate to see thirst playing on your mental equilibriums,"

"Do we fill them up at the tap?" asked Ludo.

Our host shook his head. "They're already ice cold."

"Thank you." Ludo glanced at me. "What do you think then, Garris? Is this a deal we want to take?"

"It depends on whether you want the information I have," Earl Henderson said. "You are, of course, more than welcome to make a run for Mr Fusby and his automobile. But if you stay, you will learn what I gave this creature, and you can learn where it was when I last had contact with it. Surely it is more than enough for me to bargain with."

I squirmed a little in my chair. "I suppose, at the moment, we have no other choice but to agree."

Ludo laughed. "My sentiments exactly. We shall do it, Earl Henderson."

The big man fixed us with both grin and sparkling eyes. "Excellent! Excellent! I am sure men of your experiences will cope with the challenge. I imagine I will be seeing you at breakfast, your faces flushed with the excitement. Then I will tell you all I can. Relate a location for your prey."

"And if we don't emerge in the morning, will you reveal this information to Fusby?"

Earl Henderson pulled himself from his throne, with a vigour which belied his age. "I will have to discuss that with whoever they send to replace you. For now, I will get a couple of my boys to drive you into my estate. The sun is setting and, whereas I have every faith in you two gentlemen, you need to watch the shadows."

CHAPTER TWELVE

Two large white guys drove us off-road into Earl Henderson's estate. They were much the same breed as those who'd greeted us at the gate (and a similar type to a small army of thugs we'd recently met on a strange private island). Wherever Earl Henderson got his men, they seemed to be manufacturing them mainly out of tattoos and muscles.

It was interesting, however, to see the way they regarded their much older employer. The aspect they took when called into his presence was close to awe. It went beyond dutiful, to near fervour. I'm sure if Earl Henderson had ordered them to shoot Ludo and me in the head, they would have done so without hesitation. It wasn't a comforting thought. Particularly as these two were in charge of driving us to who knows where to meet Lord knows what. Equally instructive was the way he looked at them. They might regard him as a cross between a father and a god, but he – in public at least – treated them with curt dismissal. An old-fashioned aristocrat dealing with an under-butler and only vaguely recalling his name. The orders came in short sentences. There was no hint of a 'please'. What's more, the light in his eyes went strangely muted. They were only going to be allowed the full expansive, beatific grin once they did their jobs properly.

Before we left, he said to us: "Gentlemen, one or two men have lost themselves a little in the darkness. They have not been able to cope with the wide sky and the empty spaces. They have been spooked. And believed as reality all the creatures their imaginations could conjure. But I am sure you are better than them. I sense it in my water having met you. If what I have heard of your Organisation is correct, then there is not much in this big and strange world which is going to scare you, is there?"

He paused, giving us a chance to speak, but leapt in before either of us could say a word.

"Other men would take this as an opportunity to boast. And whereas I would be fascinated to discover what gentlemen with your experiences might boast about, I have great admiration for those who have grasped how to retain their own secrets. Have a good night there, my friends! I am certain we will speak in the morning. In fact, I am already looking forward to it."

Fusby and the Range Rover we'd arrived in had already disappeared by the time Ludo and I emerged. The ten minutes having elapsed. Then we were on our way. In the back of an open-topped Jeep, the dirt swirling at us. Little rocks occasionally hitting the sides as the wheels churned them up.

We hadn't yet changed from the suits we'd worn in Vegas. I'd thought we were out of place in them there. British office suits from Marks & Spencer do not meld with the faded glamour of that city. Here, in another desert thousands of miles away, we couldn't have been more conspicuous if we'd been dressed in kilts and feather boas. Actually, kilts and feather boas may have been more apiece with the colonial vibe Earl Henderson gave off.

Neither of the muscular men said a word as we drove the couple of miles from the house, while staying on Earl Henderson's land. They wouldn't have been able to make themselves heard to us in the backseat, anyway.

Finally we reached the spot Earl Henderson presumably had in mind. A desolate piece of open desert, with a few shrubs and a big wide rock standing about eight feet high.

The driver slammed on the brakes, thrusting us both forward. Either he had nearly missed the drop-off point, or he wanted to shake us up and see how nervous we were.

"Are you looking forward to your evening?" asked the one in the passenger seat, a mocking grin forcing its way through his goatee beard.

We clambered, ungracefully and without enthusiasm, over the side of the Jeep.

"Yeah, you ready to spend the night under the stars?" asked the driver.

Both of them spoke in thick South African accents. The driver at a much higher pitch than I'd have imagined.

Obviously neither of them cared whether we replied.

"Yeah, look at them stars. The stars," said the passenger, as if it was a piece of doggerel he was reciting. "You've got to keep your eyes peeled for the stars."

Ludo was by far the shortest of the men present, but he rarely allowed himself to be intimidated.

"I don't suppose you'd offer us a hint, would you?" he said,

"What's that?" asked the driver.

"I appreciate the performance of it all," said Ludo. "Your boss has the voice for ghost stories. He should read them on the radio. With that chuckle permanently in his tone, his would be the type of spooky yarn where the twist is there is no ghost, and it was insurance fraud all along. *Tales of Scooby-Doo*, as it were. He has a good timbre for such things, while you two are doing sterling work in your Rosencrantz and Guildenstern support bit. But we're here, and Earl Henderson has been left miles away, so can you not provide a teaser? A little clue as to what we might be expecting."

The two of them turned to each other, both on the verge

of giggling. Either Ludo's accent, or the words he used – or maybe the predicament in which we found ourselves – was incredibly amusing to them.

"You want to make sure the bed bugs don't bite," said the driver. Then he slammed his foot to the accelerator, and the Jeep was gone in yet another cloud of dust. The two of us stood in its wake, coughing and shielding our eyes.

When I'd regained my composure, I stared around some more. It seemed this was a clearing Earl Henderson – or one of his lackeys – had put more than a little effort into. It wasn't as craggy as ten feet further away, nor did the spiky shrubs grow so fulsome. I realised there was a circle of rocks around us. Half buried in the sand. None of them were particularly big, no more than a foot high or wide. They weren't going to keep anything out. In fact they might advertise where we were. A goat being tethered for a lion in exactly the same spot day after day.

Ludo finished coughing, and then asked me: "Could I have a drop of your water please, Garris?"

"Where's the flask Earl Henderson gave you?"

He shrugged. "I seem to have left it behind. Must have been in the hallway when we were making our exit."

I reached into my inside jacket pocket and retrieved the silver cylinder, handing it to him. He unscrewed it and took a small sip, swilling it around in his mouth. Then he spat it out.

"I think it's just water," he said.

"You suspected something stronger?"

"A lot stronger." He passed the flask to me. "With his talk of how some men went insane, while others didn't, I expected him to be slipping in hallucinogenics. That we'd be here looking at the pretty pictures our fingers made when we waved them in front of our eyes."

"But having tasted it, you don't think so?"

"I trust my palate. And I'm pretty sure it's just water."

"Good," I said, and took a big gulp. Not spitting out mine.

And there we stood, two silhouettes under the slowly sinking sun.

CHAPTER THIRTEEN

"What do you think?" Ludo asked.

"What do you mean?"

We were sat on the desert floor, our backs to the large central rock. The air becoming progressively cooler around us.

"About what Earl Henderson has in store for us," he said. "If we haven't been slipped hallucinogenics, then whatever it is must be real and tangible and able to hurt. Or else, I suppose, it's the other way, and he's making it all up."

"He could have put them in our beer," I said.

"And yet, I don't believe he did."

"What are you thinking?"

"It could be he is a storyteller. He tried to chill us to our bones with his words, and is going to see – over this long and dark night – whether we give in to irrational fear. There are lions out there that might come near us, but really it's unlikely. This is a gigantic space, after all. So, this is a test of our mental fortitude. Whether we let our imaginations get the better of us, and arrive at his house tomorrow gibbering wrecks. Or instead, we prove to him we can conquer our own created fears."

"Unless a lion wanders in here?" I suggested.

He gave a mirthless chuckle. "That's the wildcard element of it all. He would want the whiff of real danger in the mix as well."

It was incredibly quiet. We both lived in capital cities and so never, in our daily lives, experienced this level of silence. There were only our voices, and the occasional (very) distant cawing of a bird. We spoke in hushed tones. Not wanting to damage the peace.

"But if it's mainly a test of our mental fortitude, then we can do this," I said. "We have obviously been in far scarier situations."

"Yes, and that's what worries me most. He knows of The Organisation and he thus has an idea who he's dealing with." Ludo fixed his gaze to the far horizon. Possibly hunting for something – anything – moving in the increasing gloom. "He obviously wants to put fear into us, so perhaps he isn't bluffing. If he was bluffing, he would be bigger and more expansive in his descriptions. He wouldn't be coy. Or he'd be coy enough we could guess what was here. It'd be a case of letting our own guess frighten us."

"You think whatever it is actually is real then?"

He chuckled. "I am talking myself into it, aren't I? I do, as of this moment, believe there is a genuine threat here. The more I consider it, the greater is my conviction that it would be unsporting of him *not to* have an actual creature. He's a man who lives by a code, and no matter how strange the code might be, I suspect subterfuge isn't part of it. I think, if he was going to slip us drugs, he would tell us openly and honestly beforehand. He would take great pleasure in watching our reactions as we forced ourselves to swallow whatever he'd given us. For Earl Henderson, it would be part of the game. And we'd be cowards if we didn't accept the rules of his game. But the way he's hemmed and hawed about what was here, says to me it is something real. This isn't only a test of our fortitude. There's definitely a thing out there, but for his own self amusement, he doesn't want to tell us what it is. What about you, Garris? What do you think?"

I took a sip of water. "Unfortunately, I agree with you. So what are we thinking here? Strange and esoteric and only stalks forth after dark?"

"As Fusby said, vampires and werewolves are the two which readily spring to mind. Yet how would he be able to control either of those? Vampires have minds of their own. They also have very good survival instincts. No vampire would want a load of blood-drained corpses showing up in Botswana. It would raise too many questions. As for werewolves…"

"It's possible," I shuddered. Not long ago I'd had a terrible experience with a werewolf in Scotland. While more recently, I'd come to believe I had a werewolf within me. Ready to burst its sharp canine teeth through my skull. It was a fear which still surfaced in most of my nightmares.

"But," Ludo said, "werewolves soon learn they don't need to change under the full moon. They have more willpower than the myths give them credit for. If werewolves are here, then they would have as much control over Earl Henderson as he would over them. His army of goons couldn't stop one in a rage. Particularly if the lycanthrope was clear minded and directing its hunger. But then, what else could this thing be?"

"Whatever it is, I have the distinct feeling it's going to be coming soon."

The moon was rising, and was indeed full, which did not ease my nerves. I was about to take another sip of water (wishing now it was something stronger), but then stopped myself. We only had the one flask. It was best to ration it.

We watched the sky and the horizon for a long while, waiting for movement, but nothing happened.

There was the caw of more than one bird in the distance. A gentle breeze occasionally made the shrubs rustle yards beyond our stone circle. But there was nothing to alarm us as yet. The sky was clear, and the moon higher. There seemed to be thousands of stars overhead. In other circumstances it might be considered beautiful. Such was the brightness, I'd have thought we'd be able to see anything approaching for miles around. But instead it was as if shadows were swallowing our surroundings. Everything beyond our immediate circle was lost in an ink-stained preternatural gloom.

Neither of us said anything further. Nor did we move. Sitting as still as statues, we listened and waited and didn't glance at our watches to see how much or how little time had passed. It didn't matter. We were here until the sun rose and that was going to take as long or as short a time as it did.

As the minutes – maybe hours – went by, I started to wonder whether Ludo's initial theory, that Earl Henderson was trying to scare us, was actually correct. It felt increasingly plausible. This was a ruse. We'd emerge cold and stiff and tired in the morning, and he'd laugh at the sheer credulity of two men from London who worked for The Organisation, falling for his rumbly-toned scare tactics.

Rather than being frightening, it was instead going to be a tedious night.

But then the growl came. It emanated from a creature both big and hungry. Somewhere out there, in the shadows that seemed to evade the moonlight.

Ludo and I scrambled to our feet and pressed our backs against the largest rock. We exchanged looks of concern; at times like this, we tended to think alike. It was difficult for the two of us, unfamiliar with this landscape, to grasp exactly where the sound originated. But it sounded far too near.

Neither of us said a word or made a sound. The worry was how far a whisper might carry in this exposed environment.

Within a minute, there was a second growl.

Whatever this creature was, it was suddenly a lot closer. Between this growl and the last, it had pelted towards us. Or else, and this was the more horrible scenario to consider, there was more than one of them. I froze with the cold rock at my spine and listened as hard as I could. Straining to hear the padding of feet on the ground. Or hungry panting coming nearer. I listened for other wildlife, in case I could hear anything doing its best to get out of the way. But the other animals would probably be fine. By far the biggest prey here was Ludo and me.

A dozen regrets went through my mind. Primarily that we'd taken Earl Henderson's challenge, and not tried to wheedle the information from him another way. Or else that we hadn't waited around in this spot for whatever this creature was to come for us. Right from the start, I'd held the image of a goat staked, and yet I hadn't broken the metaphorical rope and fled into the wilderness. But where else would we realistically have gone? We could just as easily be running through the dark at this second, wishing we had stayed where we'd been. At least our backs were protected by the solid rock.

Ludo squeezed my arm, I think in a reassuring way. It was at that exact same instant the beast growled again. It was so close. I could almost hear it breathing.

When I looked at him, there was a determination to survive sparkling in Ludo's eyes. I was glad to see it. It gave me resolve. He met my gaze and pointed his index finger upwards. It was all we had, the only plan remotely on offer, so it was the one we had to grasp.

We simply had to hope the creature couldn't climb.

Ludo reached his hands and nodded to me when he'd found something to grab onto, then I pushed him. Getting him off the ground and then following. Putting my feet and hands in exactly the same places, and letting my extra height do the work. Together we hauled ourselves upwards as fast as we could. Of course there was no way we could do it quietly. There was straining and huffing and puffing. But then the beast absolutely knew where we were and was coming for us. Maybe it would give it a little thrill to hear our desperate scrabbling to escape.

With a wheeze and a grunt, Ludo reached the flat top first and spun himself around to help me. I grabbed on tight to his hand and hauled myself the remaining few feet, almost landing on top of him. Then I stared down.

I expected a wolf. One as big and grey as that which had haunted my dreams. Instead, when the creature strode languidly into the clearing, I didn't bother to stifle a gasp.

It wasn't a wolf; it was a kind of lion. A big yellow feline, as big as a man.

And as it snarled at us and licked its lips, I saw its eyes were red with fire.

CHAPTER FOURTEEN

Once the creature had stepped into the circle, there was no question that it was in charge. It slowly padded around on its huge paws. Unhurried. As if knowing it wouldn't have to expend much energy to kill us. This was no longer the place we were hiding, hoping it wouldn't come near. Now it was where it was going to toy with us until we died.

We were alone. There were no other people for miles around. Apart from the ones who had put us in this creature's path. So it could take its time with us. If it wanted to tear off one of our arms and then bathe in our spurting blood, then there was going to be very little we could do to stop it.

The sleek muscularity of its frame and its yellow fur should have identified it as a lioness. Except its genitalia absolutely marked it as male. Besides which, this close, you could see it was not a lion of any kind. Its face was longer and sharper than I'd ever seen on nature documentaries. Its ears were heavier and hung down the side of its face; while its eyes were enormous and glowed with the flame of a furnace.

At first I'd thought the glowing eyes were a trick of the

light. That this creature's irises were tinted a certain shade which made the silvery moon reflect as red. But the glow was still there when it stared down as well. The redness reflecting onto the soil, as if each eyeball was a small torch. There was fire inside it. This was a walking and growling animal, which was a volcano. For the moment, it was relatively calm, but if pushed, it would undoubtedly erupt. The creature gave a low growl from the base of its throat. A rasping sound of control. Probably more to warn off its brethren, than to scare us. But I couldn't help hear the edge of impatience within it. Hunger and impatience.

And from somewhere in the darkest corners of my mind came an answering growl. One that belonged just to me.

I did my best to pretend it wasn't there.

There wasn't a lot of room at the top of the rock. Ludo and I were eight feet high and crammed together, my leg looped over his. As intimate as we had ever been with each other. Surely this animal couldn't jump high enough to get us. But it was going to be a painful evening staying cramped in that position.

"What on earth do you reckon it is?" asked Ludo, in almost excited fascination. He whispered. In fact we both whispered. It was strange as this creature couldn't be any more aware of us.

"I don't know. A big cat. I have no idea what kind."

"Its tail is shorter than most big cats," he said. I hadn't noticed the fact, but he was right. Its tail was a stump, a third as big as it needed to be for its frame. "Also it's huge. Much bigger than any other cat I've ever seen."

"Whatever it is, it's not native to Botswana."

"I think we would have heard of it if it was."

The sheer size of it was demonstrated at that instant. It raised itself on its hind legs and leant its front paws against the rock. Even as high as we were, its talon-like claws were only a foot or so below us. If it sprang (*when* it sprang) we were going to be easy meat to sink its teeth into.

"What the hell are we going to do?" I wailed.

"Hand me your flask," he demanded.

"What?"

"Just do it."

It wasn't an easy manoeuvre, considering how little room we had, but I reached into my inside jacket pocket and removed the silver flask.

Ludo took it off me and hurled it as far as he could.

It bounced in the sand outside the stone circle.

The creature watched it go and, as it did, dropped onto all fours. But it didn't make any move in the flask's direction.

"What the hell did you do that for?" I snapped.

"The way Earl Henderson was so eager to give them to us, made me think there might be something more to them. Either a hallucinogenic, or a tracking device. But I suppose if it is emitting a frequency which has attracted this animal towards us, it now knows we're here and is not going to go hunt elsewhere on the off-chance."

"You don't have so huge a throw, Ludo," I told him. "Besides, if it did now follow the bloody tracker, it going to retrieve it from fifteen feet from us wouldn't offer much in the way of a respite."

"I'm sorry." He shrugged and demonstrated the precariousness of our situation by forcing me to cling on tighter. "Much to my father's chagrin, I was never much of a sportsman."

If the creature had been distracted by the flask flung through the air, the moment was gone. It let go a tremendous roar into the darkness. A roar that must have echoed right across the estate. I could imagine Earl Henderson standing in his window and listening to it, quaffing an appreciative whiskey as he did. There was a commanding dominance to the roar. It seemed to imply the creature would be busy tearing us apart for the next hour, and didn't want to be disturbed.

However, I answered it. I raised my head and howled into the sky. Feeling my skin prickle as the wolf of my dreams tried to push its way free of me.

"Easy, Garris," said Ludo.

If Earl Henderson was listening, I wondered what he made of that howl.

But the creature wasn't daunted. It pushed itself up against the rock, and I thought it was going to make the leap. Its sharp claws would slash at us, its teeth would sink into our flesh, and in our desperation to get away we'd roll off the other side and become a much easier feast as we lay injured in the dirt.

As its gaze pierced into us, it growled. And as it did, a lick of flame shot from between its lips. A splutter for now, but clearly it was capable of much more.

Ludo and I kicked ourselves from it as far as we could, and I felt the hot, putrid air go past me.

Panicked, we nearly did topple down the other side, but just as we steadied ourselves, the creature shot out its tongue.

A tongue which in no way belonged to a cat. It was long and thin and reptilian, and it lashed out and wrapped itself tight around my left ankle.

CHAPTER FIFTEEN

I screamed.

The tongue lassoed my leg, winding its way around my calf twice. Then it squeezed. There was trouser between my skin and the actual meat of the tongue, but I could feel the powerful tendons of it, nonetheless. A long vein down the middle of the protuberance throbbed with excitement. Below me, the creature's eyes blazed. Fury and hunger and naked desire intermingling.

I cried out in alarm. Another sound which Earl Henderson might have listened to with glee.

Growling from its throat, the creature began lowering itself from the rock, yanking me with it.

"Ludo!" I called in panic.

But a second later, I turned and howled at it. Swiping with claws I didn't have and trying to slice the tongue away from me.

"Focus, Garris!" I heard him yell. "There's no wolf which can emerge. You're only a man."

I blinked and regarded him, nodding to let him know there was a part of me which understood reality.

Ludo clutched hold of my arms, yet there was going to be little he could do. This creature was bigger and more powerful than him. Ludo couldn't throw a half-filled flask particularly far. He wasn't going to match this thing for strength. All it had to do was to keep dragging me and it would probably haul Ludo off the rock along with me.

"Curl your legs into yourself!" Ludo called.

For a few seconds I gawped at him uncomprehending. My legs were already dangling off the side; curling into myself meant pushing my body to the edge. Losing the little advantage I had from most of my weight being on top of the rock. But the expression on Ludo's face showed he had at least the germ of a plan. I had to trust him. It wasn't as if my feeble clinging onto him was going to save me.

It's not like giving into the wolf was going to save me either.

Taking a deep breath and pushing down as much of the internal fear as I could, I jack-knifed my body, so it was a bare inch from the edge. Pulling my legs and yanking the creature a little towards me.

It growled in irritation, a strange noise which – since its tongue was wrapped around my leg – vibrated through me.

I lay on the brink. Nearly toppling into the desert below.

But then I saw what Ludo had in mind.

Still clutching my hands, he got as close to the edge as he could and lashed out with his foot. Hitting the tongue where it was wrapped around me. Both it and my ankle shuddered.

The thing didn't let go, however. In fact it tightened, so I could feel it almost through to my fibula. I was sure my foot was turning blue.

"I'm sorry if that one hurt you, Garris. I shall do better."

He raised his boot and stamped, connecting with the protuberance. Only this time below where it reached my leg, so there was solid stone beneath it.

The creature emitted a roar which was both pained and outraged. Sensing he was on the right path, Ludo stomped again. But this time, the creature jerked its tongue at the last instant and the blow crunched me in the knee. I gave a gasp of pain, before howling into the night sky.

"Sorry about that, old man," said Ludo. "Please do your best to stay with me."

He tried again. This time his aim was true and, more importantly, it was hard enough for the beast to think twice.

I felt the world sway in front of me for an instant and vomit rise to my throat. But equally there was relief as the tongue let go and jerked away from me.

The roar of fury the animal released was almost deafening.

And I tried to match it in my wolf-howl of response.

Ludo and I scrambled together to a more secure position atop the rock, but the world around me was swaying and the sky was becoming a rich blood red.

"It's in my skull, Ludo!" I cried. "It's been there a long time, and it's desperate to take control!"

Ludo gripped my hand. "If you were an actual werewolf, I'd almost be inclined to let you go. If you could scare it off, then I'd only have the one beast to deal with. But you're not a wolf, you're a man. If you jump on that thing, you're not going to overwhelm it with your lycanthrope strength. No, you'll be torn apart."

"I can't stop it!" I yelled. It was engulfing every inch of me. Fur and fangs ready to burst through my flesh.

But Ludo had become distracted from me.

"Oh no!" he murmured. His eyes fixed on the creature.

Almost not wanting to see, I peered over the edge. There was a bubbling at its spine and it was tossing its head around wildly. We were too experienced to be lulled into false hope, but you could almost believe there was something wrong with it. However, there were no accompanying whimpers of an animal injured. The look on its face did not suggest it was suffering. Instead, it appeared more vicious than ever. Whatever it was doing, it was in full control.

The skin seemed to expand outwards. Its flesh growing. Twisting. The muscles of its torso split apart; its body opening. The bubbling stopped and its spine arched and the creature unfurled a wide set of wings.

It growled at us, an expression of triumph on its near-feline face.

And knowing I was going to die, the dam within me wouldn't hold. I howled furiously at the moon, shook myself free of Ludo and leapt from the top of the rock. Plunging towards the creature with my mouth open and roaring incoherently.

"*Garris!*"

CHAPTER SIXTEEN

Below us, the beast had started flapping its wings. They were so wide and heavy, it was almost distorting the air itself.

It didn't stop me. It didn't stop the wolf inside. With a scream which was almost a berserker's roar, I landed on its back.

My mouth open, I tried to bite into its side, just above the wings. I could feel the wolf within, but of course, stayed only a man. My teeth remained human teeth. I bit into its side and tasted its pelt (which was disgustingly sour).

But then with a shake, it hurled me off. I had irritated it, rather than caused it damage. Undoubtedly my fifteen stone frame would have bruised it when I collided into its torso, but I didn't do anything to cause lasting injury. I don't think I even pierced its flesh.

I landed painfully on my shoulder with a thump, and the sudden fearful realisation of what I was and what I had attempted to do now threatened to overwhelm me.

The wolf retreated. Lowering its head.

Then it was me lying in front of this creature's hungry, salivating jaws. Knowing there was nothing I could do to stop it killing me. It could burn me with its fire, or squeeze me with its tongue. And now it could fly as well as run, there was nowhere I could go where it wouldn't be able to snare me.

"Garris!" Ludo called.

My eyes stayed on the creature. I didn't glance at Ludo. I had no idea whether he had one last grand plan. It hardly mattered anymore.

For the first time since it had become part of my mind, I tried to summon the wolf, rather than banish it. To pull it from within and make it take my place. If I was going to die, I wanted to die fighting. But nothing came. The wolf hid, whimpering.

While the creature moved in on me, its eyes ablaze.

Three shots rang from the darkness.

In the desert quiet, they were like the booms of high explosive.

The creature jumped, startled and confused. None of the bullets had hit it. Although at least one had come close, punching into the rock where Ludo still watched. Yet the creature must have understood this meant it was no longer the dominant force.

It had its sharp teeth, its burning eyes, the ability to spout fire, that tongue and now it had wings. If we'd let it work through its bag of tricks, who could fathom what else it might be capable of? But it also had brains and understood not to mess with any man wielding a gun. It backed away from me and stood in front of the rock, the stretch of its newly found wings longer than its entire body length. Then it peered into the desert for this unfamiliar presence. Perhaps wondering if there was a way for it to regain the upper hand. If it could get a sight of its new assailant, perhaps it could climb high and then swoop in blasting flames. Make the gun an utter irrelevance as it reclaimed its position as the alpha.

For half a minute, there was no noise. Lying there helpless, I almost started to believe the shots had been a group hallucination between me, Ludo and the animal. Or our would-be rescuer had only brought a trio of bullets. But then another one burst through the air. It missed the creature, and it was clear whoever was firing, wasn't aiming at it. He was only attempting to scare off this strange winged cat.

But he wasn't succeeding. As the shot echoed around us, the animal emitted a roar: ~~high~~ high pitched and piercing. Nothing close to the sound of an enormous cat, or even a wolf. And then it began to beat its wings. Undoubtedly its eyes were far better than mine when it came to seeing into the darkness. I couldn't make out a thing, but it fixed itself on a particular spot and lifted its entire frame from the ground. The sound of those big heavy pinions cracked against the air. Pulsating up and down, the creature squawked at the same time. Now more akin to a bird than a mammal.

If I'd been watching it on a nature documentary – at a safe distance, where no harm could befall me – I would have been fascinated by it. This impossible creature, which should not exist, lifting its feline form into the air with wings it had grown before my eyes.

But lying in the clearing next to it, knowing the precariousness of our situation, it was impossible not to tremble. I raised my hand as a cloud of dust billowed from its launch. The animal wailed into the night sky, having raised itself six feet into the air seemingly without expending any effort. It wouldn't require much to turn around and grab hold of one of us in its claws. To take Ludo off the top of the rock as if he was Fay Wray. Dangle him in the large maw of its mouth, and then fly off to where no hero with a rifle could get to him. We were both utterly exposed.

However, it ignored us. It was concentrating on the man with the firearm. It gave another terrifying squawk and then I heard it – even above the wings – take a deep breath of air.

It sent a burst of flame towards our would-be rescuer. The sky lit up like a fireworks display. There must have been twenty feet of fire, filling the air with rage and sulphur.

Ludo took the opportunity to get himself off the rock. He slid down uncomfortably on his stomach and side, landing with a grunt. I couldn't say what his plan was. Possibly he thought that if our rescuer was incinerated, we'd make a run for it. Try to find a hole in which we could hide until morning. Up on the rock was no good; the clearing was no good. Quite probably there was nothing at all out there, but while the creature was distracted, we had to take the chance.

Another shot. But the man with the rifle had evidently decided warnings weren't good enough anymore. The bullet hit the animal in its side, whizzing right the way through. Thick purple blood splattering onto the sand in front of us.

The creature let loose another extraordinarily high-pitched scream. This one a lot more about pain than power. It spiralled in the air. To me, it looked a flesh wound more than anything else, but it was going to make it painful to walk or fly. If it was any feline which normally inhabited this planet, it would disappear to lick its wounds.

Instead, this strange winged lion continued to flap its wings almost lazily, to survey its surroundings. Perhaps not wanting to admit it was beaten, and thus making itself an easy target. The old adage raced through my mind of a cornered animal being at its most dangerous, and I wondered if this was a ruse. I waited for it to scream again, or for it to blast another burst of fire. But after a few moments, good sense must have got the better of it. This winged cat arched in the sky and flew off. Roughly, I estimated, towards Earl Henderson's home.

Still cowering on the ground, Ludo and I peered nervously and wondered whether the situation could get worse. But then our rescuer stood and showed himself. He climbed from behind a rock and strolled forward with the rifle outstretched to ward off any other predators.

And thankfully, his was a friendly face.

"Need any help, gents?" asked Fusby.

CHAPTER SEVENTEEN

"Of course, I stayed on the property," Fusby said, surprised that we were surprised. "Earl Henderson deals a lot on trust, which is interesting, as I wouldn't trust him as far as I could spit him. So I knew if I gave my word I was leaving, Earl Henderson would take me at my word. He would be unlikely to call to the gate to make sure I'd actually gone. Of course, when he learns of my deception, it will mean the 'friendship' between him and me is done. But if anything happened to you two, our relationship – such as it is – was going to be finished, anyway. It was a simple decision to make."

"What if he'd had you escorted to the gates?" I asked.

He shrugged. "Then I'd have snuck back in. Earl Henderson likes to think his perimeter is solid, but I have my ways. I work for The Organisation, after all."

Almost as much as the rifle, I was happy to see he had a bottle of water. Ludo and I both drank thirstily.

"What happened there, Garris?" Fusby asked. "Did you fall off or what? I was going to take my first shot, when you got in the way."

I grimaced.

"It falls more into the '*or what*' category of things," Ludo answered for me. "How are you feeling, Garris?"

"Okay," I said. "Even under this big full moon, I'm feeling like myself. What happened became too scary even for the wolf."

Fusby stared at me for that remark, but I didn't elaborate and he didn't ask any further questions,

He had parked his Range Rover a mile from us. While he went to retrieve it, he took the rifle and left us with a pistol. An amateur in firearms such as myself could see it wasn't a big calibre and that I'd have to get close to one of those creatures to cause serious damage. And I didn't want to be close to one of those creatures again.

Fortunately, we had no more uncanny visitors. Nothing happened, and Fusby didn't run into any trouble along the way either. He drove the Range Rover to the edge of the circle and shone the lights in at us.

"Do you have any idea what that thing was?" I asked him.

Fusby shook his head and peered at the splattering of blood, which appeared more purple and strange under the bright headlights.

"This is far from my area of expertise," he said. "We have a team which investigates cryptids, don't we? This is the sort of thing which is going to make their days. Whatever it is, it is not going to be in any child's book of animals."

"But a child's book of myth," said Ludo slowly, crouching in front of the blood. "Tell me, have you ever heard of a Manticore?"

"No." I shook my head. "It sounds like it should be an internet start-up."

Even with what we've been through, he managed a smirk.

"No, it's an ancient Persian myth," he said. "It has the body of a lion, but the wings of a bird and the sting of a scorpion. I don't recall anything about an elongated tongue or the ability to breathe fire, however. There is something from Greek myth, a Chimera, which is the body of a lion, and the head of a goat, and various other creatures jammed in there as well."

"So he's imported in a creature of ancient myth?" asked Fusby.

"Or made them. Melding them together from different long-ago tales."

The thought of Earl Henderson as a Doctor Moreau settled heavily upon us.

"We really need to speak to him," I said.

"Well, we should be quick," said Fusby.

"What do you mean?"

He shifted a little. "When you went out on the Jeep, I couldn't get too close whilst following you. I had to stay way back, or I'd be spotted. But that meant once you'd stopped, I was too distant to really know where you were. I had only a vague idea of how to pinpoint you in this landscape. So, I found this clearing by following the creature. I could see it on the horizon and hear its growl. But I also saw two others very similar to it. One of them might even have been bigger. They were milling about, but then they roared into attention and started racing. Those other two started in the direction of Earl Henderson's home. Obviously I couldn't call ahead to warn him, as I wasn't supposed to be here."

I stared at Ludo. "You were right. There was something about the flask, wasn't there?"

"What do you mean?" asked Fusby.

"Earl Henderson gave us both a flask," Ludo said. "I thought that there might be something in it, emitting a signal to attract the animal. Garris's is over there, as I threw it to see if I could distract the creature. I did. For three seconds."

"So, why does Earl Henderson have creatures at *his* house?"

"Because only I took my flask," I said. "Ludo left his behind."

"I may have mislaid it in the cloakroom. Or stashed it in a place really hard to find."

"Right. I get it. If there's something in there Earl Henderson switches on," Fusby said. "A high frequency those creatures respond to, then they would have followed it to his front door."

"Exactly. And once there, it wouldn't matter if the signal was switched off, they'd have the scent of prey."

We peered into the distance, but it was too far to discern anything. We listened for screams or other signs of chaos, but there was nothing. Until suddenly there was something.

Distantly, being blown the wrong way on the wind, was the boom of a gunshot.

"Come on," said Ludo, jumping to his feet. "As guests, it would be churlish not to help."

CHAPTER EIGHTEEN

We didn't have to drive far to witness the pandemonium ahead. The route Earl Henderson's men had taken us was (quite deliberately) circular. Designed to confuse. Fusby drove straight, so we could see it ahead of us within a couple of minutes. It was the only building for miles around and impossible to miss, but doubly so now. There were flames in at least half of the windows. Outside, a man ran wildly into the estate, seemingly not caring where he went. Another was firing bullets into the carcass of one of those animals. Surely it must have been dead, but given all the things we'd seen one of those things do, I could understand his thoroughness. This man, with the flames licking at him from the house, took the time to crack open his automatic, reload and fire again. As we drew closer, we could hear his continuous screaming above the weapons' reports.

Earl Henderson wasn't immediately visible. The man with the gun wasn't him. He was too young and slim and short. Nor had Earl Henderson been the man who ran away. Those were the young guys who'd looked at Earl Henderson with such adoration and lived off his largesse. I'm sure, in amongst their terror, they must also feel they were letting down Daddy.

Fusby pressed his foot to the accelerator and bounced us over the terrain. This time I seemed to have found myself in the backseat and clutched on to anything around me, while keeping my eyes locked on the burning house.

When we got there, the battle was largely done. The bullets being expended were amongst the last to be fired, and there were five bodies of those creatures lying in or around the burning bricks. Obviously there'd been others that Fusby had missed. There was the one the young man had been repeatedly shooting at; while another was lying half-in and half-out of a ground-floor window. Its corpse serrated on the glass, its purple blood running down the bricks below. A third was lying directly in front of the main entrance: it was headless.

Finally we saw Earl Henderson. He was pulling a large Ottoman sword from another and dumping the carcass on top of a sibling. There was an air of grim triumph to him. Yet it didn't remove the annoyance from his face.

He was barking orders over the crackling of the flames. Some of the young men were being instructed inside to rescue items that were precious to him.

It took him a few moments to register that we'd arrived, and when he did, a certain hardness settled onto his features. A stillness returned to his frame. When he'd been yelling at his young men, his animation had been unmistakable. But once he fixed on us, it was as if he froze. He might have wanted to, but he didn't present us with a poker face. His disdain was unmistakeable.

I wondered how quickly he was putting it altogether. Whether he'd already concluded that the reason those hybrid creatures had attacked him, was one of us had been kind enough to leave a flask behind.

Ludo leapt from the car with an enthusiasm which seemed more than a little out of place in the presence of an actual burning house.

"Earl Henderson!" he called. "It seems you're having

issues here tonight. Is there anything we could perhaps do to help?"

Our host's lips pursed, and he peered at the little man in front of him. By then Fusby and I were at Ludo's shoulders, and all of us earned a cruel twist of the man's lips.

"Mr Carstairs," he said, his tone suggesting he was trying his best to force hospitality into his voice. "I was not expecting to see you until sunrise. That was our bargain, was it not? The two of you – *only* yourself and Mr Garris – would spend the night on my estate, and we would see how you survived. But you have come back early, so I assume our deal is off?"

Ludo shrugged. "Or we have a different deal. A question for you first. Why?"

"*Why?*" This time, there almost seemed to be a genuine humour in his tone.

At that instant, one of the young men ran from the house, a painting under each arm. He was shirtless and the smoke stained his muscular torso. It was surreal. The conversation Ludo and Earl Henderson were engaged in was confrontational, but politely calm; while the young man was almost frantic. His exertions seemed to be taking place in a different world to ours. "I got these, Earl Henderson!" he called, in a breathless South African accent.

"Good boy!" said Earl Henderson, not taking his eyes from Ludo. "You know what to get next."

The young man nodded. He appeared a little crestfallen to be asked once more to charge into the blaze, but didn't hesitate. Presumably he hoped he was making his father figure proud, but Earl Henderson didn't offer so much as a glance in his direction.

"Yes, why?" continued Ludo. "Why not simply hand us the information? You are fully aware what we are, you understand what The Organisation does, why invite unnecessary attention upon yourself? You could have passed us what we wanted, told us to do a good job with it, and it might have been years before anyone bothered you."

"You survived, did you not?" The big man glanced at Fusby. "I am not quite sure I appreciate the manner in which you survived, but you did."

"What was the game from your point of view?" asked Ludo. "Surely, if we had died tonight, you would have invited endless trouble upon yourself."

He gave a wheeze of a chuckle. Either for effect, or because the smoke of the fire was getting to him.

Ludo pressed him: "If we'd died, then our colleagues would have swarmed this place. Now, since we survived, the very nature of our report is going to ensure our colleagues are swarming this place. So why bother?"

Turning his great shoulder, Earl Henderson took another look at the ruined house and put his hand on Ludo's arm. It was a friendly gesture, rather than a prelude to violence.

"Do you ever get bored, Mr Carstairs?" the big man asked. "Truly and utterly and existentially bored. Oh, I get bored. Wherever I am, whatever I do, whomever I am with – I find it all tedious. Whichever lady I am making love to, I always wind up utterly bored. Crushed by the tedium of it all. I have built myself a utopia here. I am in the contact books of the most interesting people alive. Anyone rich who wants an item strange or esoteric, eventually comes to me. My life is the life I craved. The existence of a junior king. But I am bored. Magnificently bored."

Ludo smirked. "So you decided to capsize it then?"

"Why not?" He chuckled. "What is anything if you cannot lose it? How can it have value if it is yours forever and ever? It is simply yours. And there is no excitement without risk."

"So you put us there hoping you might destroy yourself?" I asked.

"I could not guess how things would conclude. You may have thought you saw nothing more than a lion with strange features. He might have sniffed you and gone away. I try my best, but in common with all felines – or *near* felines – these animals have capricious natures." He peered sadly at the two dead creatures at his feet. "One could never be certain what they might do."

"What were they?" Fusby asked.

Behind Earl Henderson, part of the roof finally collapsed.

There were cries of surprise and alarm, but nobody seemed to have been caught underneath it.

The man who owned the house didn't glimpse in its direction.

"Ha!" he said. "Well, I have never formally bestowed them with a name. Would you like to be the man who does that for me, Mr Fusby? We could call them The Fusbians, perhaps? Or The Traitors? I find things become a lot less mystical once they have a name. Of course, when I am supplying items which are truly unique, I have to name them, but it is always such an unexciting prospect."

He finally turned and stared at his house. The fire had spread across the entire length of it. The roof was pretty much gone, but I imagined the brickwork was going to prove sturdy. I could see it in the months and years ahead, scorched and blackened and abandoned in the middle of nowhere. A house out of which people conjured witches' tales.

"What next, Earl Henderson?" yelled one of his young men.

But Earl Henderson waved his hand in dismissal. Before we arrived, he had been agitated about getting his possessions, but now he merely barked: "I have already told you the once."

His attention returned to us, but there was a sadness and disdain.

"You made those creatures?" asked Ludo.

"You bred them from lions, perhaps?" I added.

Concern creased his brow. "I may be a monster, gentlemen, but I am not *that kind* of monster. Have you never seen a lioness? You must have on the television. A magnificent creature to hunt. An incredible challenge. Of course, once you have hunted a lioness, there are few other places to go. However, once you have hunted one, then you have too much respect to mess around with their natures,"

"So what are they?" I asked.

The young men were no longer going into the house. Not even the last one he'd snapped at. They didn't seek permission or approval from Earl Henderson, they simply stopped and knew they'd have to deal with his disappointment later. It was the right decision. Even at our distance, the heat was almost blisteringly, unbearably hot.

"They come from another world," he said. "From a world much like ours, and planes much like these. A world which would be too terrifying for most men to step into, but which I could offer a brief taster of. A place which needs magic to enter."

"Another dimension?" asked Ludo.

He shrugged. "I will tell you *all* you want to know." He lowered his voice and spoke confidentially. "But we have to arrive at an agreement. Obviously my time here has come to an end, but it does not mean I want to spend the rest of my life in one of your holding cells in London. Or being sailed around the world on that prison ship of yours. Oh no!"

All three of us kept admirably straight faces. None of us showed surprise that this man would have learned so much about how The Organisation worked.

"I will tell you what you want to know regarding The Ravens Creature, and I will give you the entire chapter and verse as to what I have been up to here. But we are going to have to reach an accommodation."

A smile creased Ludo's cheeks. "Your house is burning. Do you feel you're in an excellent position for a negotiation?"

"It is not my house anymore, Mr Carstairs. As with all the gambling I have done, and the other grudges against me I have stored up, possession of this house has gradually trickled away through my fingers. Once upon a time this place *was* mine. Now the banks own most of it. There are men who may come after me one day to slit my throat, because I owe them money too. Or have been too free in my attentions towards their wives or daughters. There are a thousand risks on a daily basis, and that is the way I want it. *You* could have been a risk too far. But all being well, we would have come and rescued you before anything fatal happened. Or we would have done if we hadn't become distracted here." He looked towards the house and gave the wheeze of a chuckle. "You would have survived."

"What did you supply The Ravens Creature with?" I asked.

"Nothing as dangerous as the thing he already is. Do not worry, gentlemen, my moral compass may be somewhat askew, but it does not make good business sense to sell high explosive to a madman." He chuckled mirthlessly. "If I were you, I would look on the island of Lliharne."

"And where's that?"

He'd said it in a tone which suggested the island was well known. He might have been said saying Lanzarote or Malta. Now he revelled in our ignorance.

"Oh yes! I forgot how unfamiliar you Britishers tend to be with your own little islands. It is an island off the west coast of Wales. A tiny place. Desolate and rocky. But there is a house there. An old house which long ago saw a great deal of blood. It is the perfect spot for the creature you are hunting. Remote and with history."

"And that's where he is?"

"It is where I sent the item he ordered. Whether he is still there, who can say? You will have to knock on the door."

"Thank you, Earl Henderson," said Fusby.

The big man gave him a broad smile, the first time he'd unleashed it since we'd returned to find fire. "You have disappointed me tonight, my friend. But then, I suppose, if it was the choice between following an arbitrary rule and helping a friend, I would almost certainly have done the same." He turned fully towards the house and gave a shudder even as he continued smiling. "You cannot hold on to anything forever. People think when they have a house, when they have invested in the bricks and mortar, it is theirs for eternity. But the end always comes, for either you or it. Sometimes it is best to let things burn. Survival is a state of mind."

He turned away from us, seemingly intending to stand there for a long time, the flames flickering in his eyes, watching while the fire burned and his men slipped off into the darkness.

But Ludo had one more question:

"Tell me, how do we compare to Paul Raeker?"

For a good minute, it seemed Earl Henderson was too deep in his reverie to answer. But then he gave a full, genuine laugh from deep in his stomach. "You measure up well. He was an underhanded bastard too!"

CHAPTER NINETEEN

W e left Earl Henderson in the custody of the police.
Colleagues of ours were already on the way from
London to pick him up. They'd be handling his
debrief. As much as Ludo and I wanted to speak to him
further, it'd have to wait. At dawn, Fusby drove us to the
nearest airfield. This time I managed to bag the front seat.
Although on this return journey, Fusby's driving was a lot
more sedate. It could have been all his adrenalin was
expended. That being said, he did regularly hit seventy miles
an hour, but there wasn't the sense of life and limb in peril
there had been the day before.

He took us to a café en route to the airfield, and we
grabbed something called *vetkoek*, which was a bit like a hot
sandwich; and a dish more resembling porridge, called
dikgobe. The owner knew Fusby. The two of them beamed
at each other and asked about each other's wives. I wouldn't
be surprised if Fusby had made friends with half the
business owners in Gaborone. That they all gave him extra
portions *gratis*.

The last time we'd eaten was a similarly snatched meal
of burgers and fries before we boarded the flight in Vegas.
Now it was a rush to fill our bellies on another continent

ahead of boarding a plane. The food was delicious and the cola I had – particularly sweet – was the boost I needed.

"Thank you," I said to Fusby, as he rushed us towards the airport.

"No problem, man," he said. "I'm not going to send you guys off hungry."

"Mostly I mean thank you for last night," I told him. "I like to think of us as a resourceful team, but I can't say what we would have done if you hadn't shown up."

"We'd have been burnt and eaten," said Ludo, matter of fact. "Well, maybe you'd have found the strength to wrestle one, Garris, but it would have won. Without someone coming to rescue us, we were goners. There's no way around it."

"You'd have found a way," Fusby said. "I have confidence in the two of you."

I tapped his arm, despite his faith being misplaced.

"What's this Wales place like, anyway?" Fusby continued. "When I came to Britain, the only locale I visited was London. I didn't go to Scotland or Wales, or any part of the rest of England."

"It's where Garris met his lady love." Ludo grinned. "So he should answer."

"It's very wild and pretty," I said. "But it's also quite mystical. There's a lot there of myth and folklore, stuff hidden in plain sight which most people cannot see. People think of Ireland as being the country for that, but Wales has it as well."

"And Scotland surely?" Fusby said. "I saw *The Wicker Man* recently. The ending turned my stomach a little, I don't mind saying. It was worse for my wife. I'd half convinced her it was a documentary." He beamed.

Ludo laughed. "The entire British Isles are a place of mysticism and magic. Going back to the days of Arthur and continuing with the divine right of kings. They say the line of succession comes from God, but that's another way of saying it's a sword borne from a lake. The monarch's coronation involves sitting on something called *The Stone of Destiny*. The strangeness of the whole thing is hardly hidden. It's a country which revels in legend, and it's where Jacob Ravens is from. Even if he spent most of his life away, it's not much of a surprise he's returned there now he's dead."

"I wish I could come with you," said Fusby.

I smiled. "Given what happened last night, we could do with you."

"No, seriously. A lady named Baxter, and a man named Mulhane are arriving at Gaborone Airport at noon, and I've got to get them. Do you know them?"

"They're excellent agents," Ludo said. Although Baxter had her own arrogance which Ludo always clashed against, and neither of us knew Mulhane too well. "I bet they're annoyed we got the chartered plane for our journey."

"If I didn't have to do my duties here, I'd be with you."

"Hopefully this time we'll return in one piece without needing any help," I said.

We pulled up at the private airfield and found the main gates were closed. I hopped out and pressed the buzzer. The pedestrian gate opened without a word. Pulling it towards me, I stared at the other two, but Fusby didn't seem to be surprised.

"There are three of them who run this place – son, father and grandfather. Kgalefa, Modise and Oba. If one of them needs to have a cigarette or answer a call of nature, then it all becomes a bit chaotic. They know my car. They know my face. And they know I am bringing you here."

"Fair enough," said Ludo. He climbed out behind me. "It's not a far walk to the actual runway, is it?"

Fusby shook his head. "Look at this place."

Thirty feet ahead of us was a large hangar, and directly behind it – the only part of the property not covered in sand – was the runway.

"I'm sure you can make it by yourselves." Fusby laughed. "Best of luck, gents!"

The Range Rover turned and quickly disappeared. We

waved after it.

It was then Ludo's phone rang. He showed me the screen. It was The Chief.

We went through the gate and Ludo answered. Of course we couldn't discuss Organisation business on a normal landline-to-mobile connection, so we had to go through all kinds of clicks and beeps of security to get to a link where we could talk freely.

"I've had our research team dig into this island of yours," The Chief said without preamble. "It is technically owned by a company called Jacem Holdings. It was gifted to that company seventy years ago, and it has been uninhabited since then."

"So around the time Jacob Ravens died?"

"Correct. Certainly no planning applications have been put in with regards to the place. While if it has heating or electricity or a phone, then they're not paying anything for it."

"Jacem," Ludo mused.

"It could be a mash-up of Jacob and Emilia?" I suggested.

Ludo's grin showed how impressed he was. "It could be. It could very well be. Can you discover more about this company, Chief? Anything else they own?"

"Already tried," The Chief told us. "They're a fairly shadowy bunch and we were swiftly lost in a maze of Swiss bank accounts. They've had decades to cover their tracks, but we will keep trying."

"So what of the house?" Ludo asked. "Earl Henderson said there was a history of blood there."

"Murder," said The Chief. "That's where the blood comes from. Only one house sits on the island. In 1931, a retired Oxford don named Montague Thorpe moved there, along with his young wife, who was forty years his junior."

"Forty years?" I said.

"He appears to have been a confirmed bachelor who lost his head suddenly over a pretty young thing. He was a philosophy professor, but moved there to have time and space to perform the scientific experiments which were his hobby. The newspaper reports in the aftermath of the incident are frustratingly imprecise as to what those experiments were. Anyway, their wedded sojourn did not last long."

"What happened?"

"She killed him three months after they arrived. What exactly transpired isn't clear. Once more, the local newspapers are letting us down. Only this time it isn't a lack of precision, it's a falling onto old stereotypes. The young bride's – Petula Glascock, her name was – hysterical nature is commented upon. That is seen as enough to explain the whole tragedy. The remote location, plus a woman who was highly strung were a recipe for disaster."

"But you think there's more?" asked Ludo.

The Chief cleared his throat and lowered his voice, as if someone who had cracked through all the layers of security which surrounded this call could be foiled by him edging to a murmur. "The thing is, and I didn't realise this until I ordered the digging this morning, we have a file on this house. The newspaper reports are in it, yellowed now. But they would have been yellowed when they were placed in there. There's a note that the case needs to be looked into further, written by Paul Raeker himself."

Ludo and I shared a glance. Paul Raeker again. As Earl Henderson had correctly said, he had been the first agent The Organisation hired at the end of The Second World War. He'd been crucial in setting the remit and the infrastructure of the body, and was close to a legend in our circles.

"I'm guessing no one got around to looking into it further?" I ventured.

"There's nothing in his official biography to suggest Raeker did. Nor anyone else. Then, as today, there are so many *possibles* which cross our radar. Too many for us to be able to check them all."

"Can you do me a favour, Chief?" Ludo cut in.

The Chief gave a grunt which was neither yes nor no. It was non-committal and irritated at the same time.

"I read Earl Henderson's main file on one of the planes we took here," Ludo continued, "and there's nothing pertinent in there, but can you see if there's any connection between him and Paul Raeker? Earl Henderson said he worked with him."

"Did he?" For once there was genuine surprise in The Chief's voice.

"Possibly after Raeker had retired," I added.

"Still, we should have heard a whisper of it. I will have someone take a look through the records."

"Thank you."

We were nearly at the hangar, but we hadn't yet seen anyone. Fortunately there were no planes coming in.

"When you arrive back here," said The Chief, "I'll have reinforcements available for you. You don't need to go into this just the two of you. Other agents and security officers are ready to accompany you."

We'd entered the hangar and our voices echoed in the vast empty structure. At the far side was a shed that must serve as an office and, perhaps, communications. Traffic control for this small airfield.

"That's very kind, but I don't think so," said Ludo, before I had had time to consider it. "We were given this lead just the two of us, and we have followed it just the two of us. Whatever is waiting for us there is going to expect just the two of us to arrive."

The Chief paused, framing his words carefully. "You sound eager to walk into a trap, Carstairs."

"Quite possibly we are," he said. "The vampire in Las Vegas. The fact the person imparting the information was Emilia Ravens herself. Earl Henderson being involved. You and he both even mentioned Paul Raeker."

"Your point?" asked The Chief.

"It feels as though something is culminating. These are

all curiosities which have been at our periphery for a while. Things an educated soul could guess would intrigue us. It seems a person – or an entity – has gone to a lot of effort to get us interested, so it would be a shame not to learn what they want."

"Although, can't we do all that with a security detail within shouting distance?" I asked.

Ludo grinned at me. "Where's your sense of adventure, Garris? You surely didn't take this job for the peace and quiet. We do it for days like this. And let's be fair, we came alarmingly close to dying last night, so another night doing anything is a bonus. And visiting creepy old houses on creepy old islands off the coast of Wales is almost a busman's holiday."

We finally reached the shed, and both of us stopped in our tracks. Behind the old oak desk at the centre, which appeared to be the office area, was the youngest of the three men who ran the airfield. He was tied to his chair. His eyes were wide and desperate. A radio was on a bench behind him. But all we could hear were the vague, muffled words coming from behind the black tape across young, groggy Kgalefa's mouth.

"Something has come up, Chief," said Ludo quickly. "We'll call you back. Give our regards to Muriel." He terminated the line.

I dashed in the direction of Kgalefa. I was going to untie him and see what the hell was going on. But then a high-pitched American voice stopped me.

"Oh, I wouldn't do that if I was you, Mr Garris."

The voice came from the shadows, and the smug and polite threat brought me up short. I thought I recognised it, but whoever it was didn't immediately show himself. He stayed hidden in the darkness of the rear of the room. I couldn't glimpse what sort of weapon he had, although I assumed he had one.

"You should do what they say and take a step back," said Ludo. I glanced at him and he had already put his hands up.

"We wouldn't want to upset Professors Albertus and Headstone after all, would we?"

The two men stepped out in long black coats, Headstone bulky and a head height and a half above his partner. But it was Albertus, of course, who was holding the gun.

CHAPTER TWENTY

"I'm impressed, Mr Carstairs," said Headstone, his voice was much what you'd expect from a man of his impressive build and size; low, rumbling and avuncular. "How did you guess so swiftly it was us?"

"*And Muriel?*" sneered Albertus, smaller and rattier and with an accent like a Brooklyn gangster's. "Does that ever work? Yes, you've alerted your blessed Chief there's a problem, but help is hours away, and we're all aware of the fact."

"You've got me," Ludo said. "As for your question, Professor Headstone. I don't know how I was so certain you were here. I should perhaps get myself tested in case I'm a low level psychic. But closer to the truth, Professor Albertus's aftershave gave him away."

A slow grin passed over Albertus's face. Its effect minimised by the gun he was holding.

The two men before us were Sons of Flambeau. It was similar to The Organisation, but with an ethos geared completely towards profit – and few qualms as to how they achieved it. Much like The Organisation, they were a highly secretive group, and so we had no real idea how many representatives they employed. These two men – both

American and both genuine academics – we had met before.

How they had found us in Botswana was not a question we were going to receive an answer to. But they tried to monitor us, just as we tried to monitor them. I got the impression they were a lot more successful than we managed to be.

Albertus's snarl marked him as a man who was possibly capable of anything, but I doubted he would have come all this way just to shoot us. So I walked to Kgalefa.

"Was this really necessary?" I asked.

"That reminds me," said Headstone. He stepped forward and jammed a silver syringe into Kgalefa's neck. The young man's eyes closed almost immediately.

"What have you done?" I yelled.

"His father and his grandfather are both asleep upstairs," explained Headstone. "I varied the dosage for the older gentleman, so it wouldn't act badly with his heart medicine. I realise you do not approve of our aims, but you cannot say we are cruel in our methods."

Ludo stared at Albertus's gun. "We may have to agree to disagree."

The little man in the black trench coat laughed and pocketed the weapon. "I trust you guys. As far as it goes, I do trust you." He pulled the visitor chair in front of the desk and sat down, casual, perhaps waiting for a secretary to bring him a cup of coffee and a small ginger biscuit. He waved his hand around for us to do the same, wanting us to be comfortable while we had our confab.

I looked at Ludo. Now they were here, we were going to have to find out what they wanted.

Headstone helped himself to the other visitor chair, while I headed to the opposite side of the shed, where I found a dusty seat on wheels, which I feared might collapse under my weight. But since there was nothing else around, I was going to have to hope for the best. Ludo perched on the corner of the desk.

Albertus asked us: "So those murders in London were

grisly, weren't they?"

Ludo sounded surprised. "Murders?"

"Come!" said Headstone. "It was a little before we met last, but we have heard of your deep involvement in the interim. We also learned, while you were investigating, you might have found information which could be of great interest to us."

We had indeed. The Sons of Flambeau were named after a monster of a man who had served The Vichy Government. He was thought to be one of the first of a new kind of supermen, bigger and stronger and more ruthless than other men. Reliable sources had it he'd been executed by his own side at the end of The Second World War, with the Allies breathing a sigh of relief. The Sons had been set up to preserve his memory and try to find other people like him. But we had discovered evidence that the real Flambeau had not died when supposed, and instead had continued to live and travel after 1945.

So far we hadn't been able to confirm this story, although it wasn't information we were going to share with these men.

"You understand we can neither confirm nor deny anything," said Ludo, giving them both a broad grin. "That's not a clever politician way of saying yes. Maybe we have something, and maybe we don't. If we do, then obviously we are never going to tell you. Any more than you would tell us. But if we don't have anything, then we wouldn't deny it. Because you thinking we have something is bound to drive you to distraction with curiosity."

"So what brings you all the way to Botswana?" I asked.

Headstone steepled his fingers in front of him. "We are here to discuss the mission you are currently embarked upon."

"The mission?"

"Your trip to Earl Henderson's home," Albertus said. "What he might have told you. Where you're heading next."

"And how would you know about that?" asked Ludo.

"Because," Albertus said, "walls have ears and people who work for the low-paying Organisation sometimes have money worries. Honestly, gents, there are office drone civil servants who have a better quality of life than you do."

"Right," I said.

"I could have much the same conversation with my bank manager," said Ludo. "But what is it you want?"

"We want to tell you to stop," said Headstone. "We want to warn you, if you continue along this path, there could be catastrophic consequences."

Ludo folded his arms and regarded both of them. "Is that a threat?"

Behind us the radio squawked. Still too indistinct and crackly for us to hear anything.

Headstone pursed his lips, which were bloodless, but the gesture came across as thoughtful rather than unpleasant. "Let us say it is a genuine warning. Not a warning where we tell you the consequences we'll be forced to inflict if you carry on with your current activities. Instead, this is a chance for us to flag up that your current path has the possibility of an awful conclusion, and you need to be aware of the fact."

Ludo grinned at me. "We were talking to our Chief in HQ when you first saw us."

"And *Muriel*," sneered Albertus. "Don't forget her!"

"And I was saying how much this whole thing seemed to be geared towards intriguing us. Making us more and more eager to get to an end. Wouldn't you agree, Garris?"

I nodded.

"Having you two show up," Ludo went on, "and say we shouldn't do anything else is the strawberry and cream on top of the trifle."

"We haven't done all this for our own amusement," Albertus said.

"No," I said. "I think you've done it to learn where we're going. Or to get ahead of us. You've given us no reason to trust you in the past. Even today you greeted us holding a gun."

For a moment, Albertus seemed like he couldn't decide what to do with his hands. As if he'd temporarily lost track of whether he was holding the pistol or not, and if he was, wanted to stuff it away and preserve his illusion of a moral character.

Headstone, however, stayed heavy and still. Despite merely sitting, his presence seemed to loom over us. "Do you think," he said, "that the widow Ravens wouldn't have been in contact with us as well? I will be honest with you, as trust is a two-way street, she has been employed as a consultant by The Sons of Flambeau for a good many years. We of course have an interest in her late husband's life and work, and she has been a great resource to us. She can't offer much on Jacob Ravens's writings, but on his life, she is invaluable."

"There are few people left alive who have met him," said Albertus. "Well, his former bodyguard is allegedly still alive, and he's apparently even older. But you know what we mean. I understand you've met a couple of particularly long-lived types yourself."

Another allusion to the murders in London, and again we stayed silent.

"So when Mrs Ravens was consulting for you," Ludo said finally, "and shared the information she gave us with you, you simply decided not to pursue it."

"She didn't share it with us," Albertus sneered. "She handed forth a lot of other information, but she didn't tell us what she mentioned to you. Much the same as her once-upon-a-time husband, she sometimes has a strained relationship with the truth. I don't think she's as tricky as he allegedly was, but who could be?"

"We've had to pick up a trail of breadcrumbs," Headstone moaned.

"And this is where the trail has led you, has it?" I asked. "Now you can take over."

"No!" Headstone was firm. "We don't want to usurp you. We cannot see the profitability in what's happening.

We're here to try and get you to stop. That's all."

Clouds had covered the sun and made the whole airfield seem colder and darker. The chill reached inside the hangar and even this shed. We could have been in Europe, rather than Africa. We might have been on the set of a monochrome movie.

Ludo grinned. "Despite my roots and despite my accent, I am a socialist. I have gone so far as to move to Copenhagen and happily pay the high income tax. I see it as the cost for the society I want to live in. But hearing you can't find the lever of profit in something does not make me believe you've discovered the joys of altruism. Instead it convinces me there's a lot you're not telling us."

"You appreciate this is and it isn't Jacob Ravens you're heading towards, don't you?" said Albertus.

"Earl Henderson called him The Ravens Creature," I said.

"And that is entirely correct." Headstone nodded. "More animal than man, and born of murder and suicide. If you go to this creature and let it do what it wants, then the results have a high probability of being devastating. That's what we're discussing, gentlemen." He regarded us both, but we kept admirable poker faces. "This Ravens Creature absolutely needs to be stopped. Nobody should go to him, and whatever bolthole he has chosen to make his own should be razed to the ground. If you venture in his direction, then we all have so much to lose."

"How?" I asked. "How is he going to spell the end of everything?"

A clock at the rear of the shed ticked by twenty seconds without either of them saying a word. They had allegedly come all this way to warn us, but they didn't want to let go of the information they possessed.

Headstone at last spoke. "He hasn't come from this world. He has no place here. None at all. The being he originally was is from here, but this new thing is from another place."

"You mean another dimensions?" said Ludo. "Until not long ago, I was sceptical such things existed, but these walls are already open. We've been on safari with creatures from there."

"I'm sure that will make a nice dinner party anecdote," snarled Albertus.

"It's best no one goes near him and inadvertently helps him with his aim," continued Headstone. "It's best to pull away. Better to call this one quits and write a nice brief report. We'll do the same. This creature wants to force open a wide bridge between this world and numerous others. And whereas I think the planet can cope with one or two wanderers between two worlds, I doubt it can survive whatever this Ravens Creature has in mind."

"You seem to have found out a lot about this," I said.

"You have your streams of information and we have ours."

"What is it that it's doing?" asked Ludo. "What are you afraid of?"

"As much as we'd love to trust you," said Headstone, without sincerity. "This is on a need-to-know basis. Suffice to say we have some expertise in this area, and have an idea of how dangerous the thing is."

A glow of realisation came to Ludo's face. In cartoons they show a lightbulb switching on above a person's head, and Ludo was the one person I'd met who exhibited something like that in real life. His face did light up. His skin seemed to glow.

"It's one of the things The Sons does, isn't it?" he said. "You've found a way to cross dimensions yourselves, haven't you? What are you doing? Exploring? Trading? Whatever it is, I bet you believe that The Ravens Creature's activities are really going to hit your bottom line."

"We know you're foolish," Albertus sneered. "But don't be obtuse."

"You underestimate us," said Headstone. "Surely you can see that giving this thing free rein has the potential to tear apart *everything*."

"Since this thing dug itself up," said Albertus, "there've been whispers, stories of things being purchased on the black, black market. The kind of arena old Earl Henderson operates within. Then there was talk that the creature was reaching for you, Mr Carstairs. It was laying a trail of breadcrumbs to lead you straight towards it."

"That's the second time you've used that allusion," said Ludo. "So we're Hansel and Gretel?"

"Yeah, you can pick which one is which," Albertus said.

Headstone nodded his head sombrely. "And we are the additional part of the fairy tale. Wherein helpful neighbours step into Hansel and Gretel's way before they reach the witch's cottage and tell them to go to their aunt's and uncle's house. Or someone else who will keep them safe. I imagine this neighbour as a man who has previously had a contentious relationship with the kids. Yelled at them when they strayed onto his lawn. Today, however, he is trying to do them a good deed."

The radio squawked, and in the distance we heard a plane. It could have been heading to Sir Seretse Khama Airport, although we understood from Fusby it was the other side of the city. More than likely it was coming for us; it was going to land at this airfield. Headstone and Albertus heard it as well. They knew our time together was limited.

"You're fully aware we have to carry on with this, aren't you?" said Ludo finally.

Neither of them said a word, so Ludo continued:

"We can't go back to our Chief and tell him that The Sons of Flambeau dissuaded us. After all, the messenger is often as important as the message. More so in this case. What you're telling us is scary, but it's also intriguing. You may be completely honest here. There is a first time for everything. But if we don't go, someone else eventually will. We'll try to stop the bad stuff, but will they? Will you, if you one day give into temptation?"

Neither answered him. They sat there looking equal

amounts of unhappy.

The radio in the corner had properly crackled to life. The pilot of the plane on final approach and receiving nothing in return. As he had not much fuel and the runway was empty, he was alerting us that he would be landing there whether we gave permission or not.

"I'm going to have to answer it," I said, getting up and moving in the direction of the radio. "I've never guided in a plane before, but I will to do my best."

Headstone too stood. Such was his size, it gave the impression the entire room altered around him. "We have tried, Professor Albertus," he muttered. "We have done our best here. All we can do from this point is let these men ponder on what we have said and hope they eventually reach the right decision. But if the two of you do go there, and you survive, then perhaps you can fill us in on the details of what you encounter."

"You are joking!" I exclaimed, as I fiddled with the dials.

"I frequently get reprimanded for not writing reports for my own bosses," Ludo said. "It seems unlikely I'll be sending one your way."

Albertus had got to his feet too, seeming more downbeat than I'd ever seen him before. "Come on, let's depart these kamikazes before it catches."

Headstone sighed. "If I hear you have survived, Mr Carstairs, then I will take myself a table in one of the bars in Nyhavn and wait for you to walk past. Then we can have a chat without any of this contentiousness. In that event, I will look forward to hearing what happened. I wish you all the best, gentlemen!"

CHAPTER TWENTY-ONE

They disappeared through the hangar doors and we didn't follow them. I did momentarily think of seeing where they went. Possibly getting the licence plate of the car they drove away in. But it wouldn't amount to anything. They were too good to allow themselves to be followed or traced.

Ludo took the receiver off me and nodded towards the unconscious young man.

I untied Kgalefa and made sure he was breathing normally. There was nothing I could do for him in the short term. We had to hope the pilots coming into land had something which would perk up him and his relatives.

Calmly, Ludo guided the plane onto the runway, not expertly, but as a gifted amateur. Certainly better than I'd have managed.

Meanwhile I found the two older men in the gantry of the hangar. They hadn't been tied, and almost looked as if they'd passed into unconsciousness after a late night's drinking session. The middle-aged son lay with his head on his father's shoulder; both snored peacefully. All Albertus and Headstone needed to do was place a couple of empty wine bottles beside them and they could have besmirched

141

their reputations.

I came down as the plane touched its wheels to the runway. Ludo and I watched it.

"Are you okay with all this, Garris?" he asked.

"What do you mean?"

"Everyone is trying to stop us from going where we're going. The Chief is suggesting he puts a battalion of soldiers behind us. And I seem to be one making the decisions. Guiding us inexorably towards whatever awaits."

"You want to do this, don't you?"

His jaw clenched and any hint of casualness about him vanished. "The original message asked for me, and so yes, I feel duty-bound to go. I'm aware it's ridiculous. At least five-eighths of my motivations make no sense. But I want to know what it is, and if someone else goes in my stead, I'll forever feel as if I'd failed a test."

"I understand." And I did. I didn't feel it with the weight he did, but I knew what he meant.

"The thing is," he continued. "You haven't been invited to this party the same way I have. Yes, we're partners and we tend to come as a pair, but if you want to exit yourself now, I'll understand. I won't drop you from my Christmas card list."

I tried to smile at him. "I wouldn't want to miss on the fun."

"Thank you, my friend. It means a lot."

"Are you worried?" I asked.

"No." His gaze moved to the plane coming to a halt. "The clouds seem more looming than they usually do, but I'm telling myself I'm not worried. How would me being worried help, after all?"

CHAPTER TWENTY-TWO

The only way to get to the island of Lliharne was on a boat. And because it was ten miles from the shore, it was too far for an amateur like me to row. Therefore, The Organisation had chartered one, along with an expert who knew these waters. And at the appointed time, a battered old fishing trawler, with its hull seemingly held together by layers of rust, came to meet us on a small, remote dock in Pembrokeshire. The boat had to be as old as I was. It had at least three broken windows and its last paint job was no doubt in my youth. But equally it appeared likely it could do the job. If it had managed to conquer these waves to this point, then surely it could manage another ten miles.

It felt odd being in Wales again. The small town where my girlfriend was raised (and where her mother still ostensibly lived) was sixty miles distant. The nearest we got to it was passing by a signpost bearing its name, after we landed at the airfield outside Swansea. Of course, I had been back there in the time since our strange encounter with the Mandrake, but never for work purposes. It felt particularly cold today. Wales always feels damp. Rain and drizzle are a way of life for the Welsh. But all the times I'd previously visited, I'd never experienced it so bitingly cold.

Fortunately they had bright yellow raincoats at the airfield for us to borrow and we put them on over our suits. The suits were exactly the same ones we had worn in Vegas. We hadn't taken them off, let alone had them dry-cleaned. We were on our third continent with them. No one had made any comments about it yet, but I doubted we were overly pleasant to be around. While we waited for the boat, we did at least get to have a cup of tea, some Caerphilly cheese on crackers, and a portion of laverbread. Ludo had never tasted it before, and I could see him steel himself as I explained it was made from seaweed. He ate it all and made polite sounds, but I got the sense he wouldn't be rushing back. It had taken me awhile to get used to the saltiness of the flavour, but since being with Beryl – who considered it the item she missed most about the land of her fathers – I'd had plenty of time to get used to it.

Finally, in the grey middle of the afternoon, the boat hoved into view.

Its captain, in fact its only crew mate, turned out to be a strikingly attractive young woman called Angharad. No more than late twenties, with resiliently fresh skin, despite the battering it must have taken from the coastal wind and rain. She was tall, pretty much six feet, slender, with long glistening red hair. Wrapped in a couple of layers, she looked lanky; but in other more fancy wear, she would undoubtedly attract the words '*lithe*' or '*gamine*'. In another life, born in a different place, she'd have been one of the beautiful people partying in Kensington and Chelsea. Maybe she would have modelled until she found her true calling. Instead, she was the only child of an old fisherman at the outer edge of Wales, and when he died, she had inherited his boat. Rather than sell it, she'd decided to make a business of it.

Angharad looked at us with bemused and amused interest. Neither of us had sea legs and so we staggered aboard. Already looking like liabilities on the water before we'd left the dock.

"You alright there, boys?" she called, her accent making it almost musical.

We assured her we were, and she chuckled at how much she evidently didn't believe us.

That afternoon, we were the only passengers. This wasn't a surprise. No one had lived on the island since the 1930s. It was almost certainly the case that whole years went by when no one set foot on this rocky outpost in the Atlantic.

The sea sprayed around us, even when we were at the dock. To save being soaked through in these days' old suits, we both joined her in the pilot's cabin, ignoring the fact that the broken windows meant we were still going to get wet. There was a small one bar fire, powered by an industrial battery. Angharad had positioned it directly in front of her legs, but most of the heat went straight out the doors and windows. It was something, however. Ludo helped himself to the seat behind her, and I stood and grabbed hold of a piece of cord hanging from the ceiling; which was either going to keep me steady, or snap in my hand and send me plummeting to the wet wooden deck. Only the next ten miles would see which.

"Are you ready then, boys?" She grinned at us.

We had told her our names, so I didn't know if she was deliberately not remembering them, or if we were such ridiculous creatures, she didn't need to remember them.

Together, Ludo and I nodded our consent. She pushed the engine into reverse and the vessel crashed backwards into the waves and then turned towards Lliharne. As we did, the rain started to pound down, crashing onto the roof. The noise akin to bullets hitting corrugated iron.

For a couple of minutes, the three of us stayed silent. Nothing we said would be heard, anyway. But gradually the storm eased, and we listened instead to the engine growling and smelled the diesel wafting through the air. I'd wondered if my stomach was going to take it, but either I got used to it quickly, or a mile or so from the coast, the waves became less choppy.

"Any particular reason you're going to Lliharne?" she asked. I knew that when our office had booked this trip, the need for discretion was mentioned. But I guessed this was all so strange to her, she couldn't hold off posing the question.

I stared at her and wondered how I could politely change the subject from what she'd asked. Ask her about herself and her life. Wonder what there was to get up to in this remote part of the British Isles.

So I was unprepared when Ludo answered: "We believe there's a man in residence there who we want to see."

"Is there?" She glanced at him, eyebrow raised. "I hadn't heard anything of anyone moving in there."

"Would you be likely to hear?" Ludo answered.

She chuckled. "You two live in London, don't you?"

"I do," I told her.

"Well, I know there no one speaks to their neighbours. The person in the flat above you can be dead six weeks before anyone notices. But we're not like that here. I wouldn't say we were friendlier necessarily, but we are more interested in the people around us. There's a woman on a farm three miles from where I live, and I pretty much know when she's ovulating. To answer your question, if someone had moved onto the island, I think we all would have heard about it. There'd be a queue on the dock of middle-aged ladies with *cawl* and *bara brith*, all hunting for an excuse to get a peek of him."

A wave hit the side of the boat and, what I feared was going to happen, happened. The cord snapped in my hand. Fortunately my legs managed to hold themselves upright, and I didn't crash to the other side of the cabin. Quickly my hand darted through one of the empty panes and clung onto the window-frame. Hoping it at least wouldn't let me down. Angharad stared at the useless cord without expression. Seemingly not angry with me for in a small way trashing her boat, nor concerned that I might become a crumpled mess on the floor.

She turned to face forward and moved the wheel almost imperceptibly, then made a strange noise in her throat. "I'd have thought, after what happened the last time someone lived there, people would think twice about choosing it as a holiday home. Or at least, they'd take a camera crew from one of those silly ghost-hunting shows."

"Yes," said Ludo. "We heard a tragic event occurred there, but I'm afraid to say we haven't had a chance to fully investigate what it was. A Professor Thorpe, wasn't it?"

"That's it. Professor Thorpe," she said. "Many, many letters after his name. He and his young wife moved there. She was smart as well. They'd met when she was one of his students, which since this was the 1930s we're talking about, marks her as a brain as well. If not smart enough to leave her husband when he went on his mad pursuit to this island."

We'd heard The Chief's precis, but it'd be useful to learn the locals' take as well.

"What happened?" I asked.

"All I can tell you are the stories you hear repeated. Apparently, in his university days, this Thorpe character was a staid academic. But as he got older, another side of his mind opened. He became a seer and a mystic. He thought he was in conversation with ghosts and goblins and all manner of things which go bump in the night." She gave a little shudder. "To you two rational London men, that no doubt seems like lunatic nonsense."

"You'd be surprised what we'll believe in," Ludo confessed.

"I'm not saying I believe in this stuff myself!" she said firmly. "I believe I have the most rational mind west of Cardiff. But it's undoubtedly the case that a lot of people gave credence to a lot of strange things. It wasn't odd for a man to be both incredibly bright, and open to the weirdest ideas. Look at *Sir Arthur Conan Doyle*" – she pronounced his entire name and title with mocking respect – "he was an author, a medical doctor and believed completely in magic."

"He believed in fairies, didn't he?" said Ludo. "Did this Thorpe believe in them too?"

She scoffed. "How do you know there are no such things as fairies? I don't believe in them myself, but I think it's a mistake to close your mind off. Wait until you see the dusk around here, the shimmering half-light. Even to a rationalist, it's clear all kinds of things could exist within it."

Ludo held up both his hands in apology. "I'm sorry," he said, "if you thought I wasn't taking you seriously. Trust me, if you say there are fairies here, we'll listen to you."

She scoffed again, but it was more of a friendly gesture this time.

"I'm not saying that," she said. "I don't believe in fairies. But people around here might, and I'm prepared to give them the time."

I glanced behind me. Already the coast of mainland Wales was far behind us. The water below was freezing and the currents would make it almost impossible to swim. It felt there were only the three of us in existence and that we were cut off from the rest of the world.

"My dad used to talk about things in the fog," she said. "He drank a lot, so who can say whether he really saw them or not? I honour his memory by giving him the benefit of the doubt. Only recently there was a very strange story in a town up the coast. Beddnic, it's called. A virus from the water, they tell us. But I've heard bizarre rumours of what it really was. I don't believe them, but it pays to keep an open mind."

Neither Ludo nor I said a word. Or moved a facial muscle. We had been there at Beddnic. It was where I'd met Beryl.

"So there are bizarre things around here," she continued, "and that's what attracted Thorpe here. To a place where there might be magic in the air. And there might be things which exist only in the fog. And there might be men who walk from the sea at night. You can see why someone who is interested in the supernatural would want a house here."

"This was 1931, wasn't it?" Ludo said.

"Around then. Not that it makes much difference when it happened. Let's say a hundred years ago, so long before my time. But I'll tell you the way I've heard it. He was a wealthy man. I don't know where he got his money from, if he was an academic, but he had the stuff. Maybe through family." She shrugged, possibly contemplating the sheer distance of such a thing from her life. "But he was the one who built the house. He hired an architect, and for months teams of builders went back and forth from here. My great-grandfather was one of the men who ferried them and I heard, such was Thorpe's generosity, the old *mun* had no need to catch any fish that summer. But then the generosity was too much, as they took advantage and dragged the job out and the house was never quite finished. Although I also heard none of them would stay there overnight, so work never began exactly at dawn. They had to wait for the first boat to head across." She shook her head. "The entire project was reliant on what time my great-grandfather finished his hard-boiled eggs breakfast."

"Have you seen the house?" asked Ludo.

She flashed her smile. "I have an idea how close I want to get to the place, and it involves staying here on this boat. When they moved in, it was to an unfinished house. He called an end to the construction and the expenditure. The walls were there and the roof, and apparently a lot of the design he wanted on the inside, but some rooms weren't finished. However, they weren't important enough to deter him apparently. Maybe he had run out of money, but, regardless, he and his wife moved in there and set up home."

"What happened next?" I queried.

"I think I'm right in saying there were a couple of months of quiet. Nothing occurred for a little while. Nobody even saw them. But then Mrs Thorpe died."

Ludo and I shared a glance.

"We thought it was the professor who died," he said.

Angharad peered through the front window, considering. We could see the island clear ahead of us.

"I can only tell you the way I've heard it," she said at last. "The way it's been told to me when anyone decided to spin a spooky tale. Do you want to hear it or not?"

"Please go on," I said.

She nodded. "As I tell it, however, it occurs to me I don't know her name. I used to hate that in school, when they'd read the fairy tales you get from *The Bible,* and there's Mrs Lot and Mrs Noah. It seemed so insulting that these women never had their own names. And here I am doing exactly the same. She was Mrs Thorpe, but it wasn't all of her. She would have been much more."

"Petula Glascock," said Ludo. "That was her name – before the wedding."

She smiled at him. "If you're aware of the story, why the hell am I telling it?"

"I'm not aware of the story, I've only been told the broadest details of it."

"How did she die?" I asked.

"I can't honestly say." Angharad shrugged. "It could be anything over there. It's so damn remote. And of course, this was long before mobile phones. Not that you're going to get anything of a reception on Lliharne. Maybe it was as simple as she cut herself and the wound got infected. Septicaemia. Or it was an illness she carried with her to the island, one she was always going to die from. Or perhaps, as the rumours suggested, he killed her. But the word went out from the supply boat which served them each week – and only ever left the goods on the dock – that Mrs Thorpe had died, and the professor had buried her on the property."

We were getting more within the tidal pool of the island, and so after a brief period of comparative calm on the water, we were hit again by choppy waves. One of them aiming so perfectly at my broken window, it was like a jug of water had been poured through onto me. We rode through it, each clinging on tight to whatever we had.

"Do you know what a necromancer is?" Angharad asked.

"Of course," we said in unison.

She half grinned in satisfaction. "I thought you would. Whatever he was teaching at Oxford wasn't spells and incantations to raise the dead, but this is what he did. His wife had died. He might have killed her. But he determined to bring her back."

"Did he succeed?" asked Ludo.

She focused her full attention on the island of Lliharne. It grew bigger and bigger before us. There was a green hillock beyond the dock and, I understood, the other side of it was a basin. A wide, rough circle of grass and the hardiest of plants. It's there the house stood. Apart from the dock, the island was pretty much unapproachable. Around it were the most jagged and the ugliest rocks I'd ever seen. They'd be a peril for the average fisherman cruising past, let alone anyone attempting to land on it. Before we left, Angharad had told us she'd headed over once or twice before. Not to ferry anyone back and forth, but because her father thought it would be useful to truly understand the dangers involved.

"Did he succeed in this reanimation?" she wondered aloud. "Allegedly he did. After a fashion."

"What do they say happened?" I asked.

"When he snatched her from death, he didn't merely bring her back. Something else attached itself to her soul. That's the theory, anyway. Although quite what happened and quite what it was, nobody knows. It was only the two of them there. Thorpe, and this thing he had brought back. The island is ten miles from the mainland, but allegedly the screams could be heard all the way clear to the nearest town. All night long the cries came. The sea was too wild for anyone to risk going immediately, and that was strange, if you think about it. How could the terror have been heard above the crashing sea? But it was and, at dawn's light, a number of the fishermen went to find out what had taken place."

"What did they find?" asked Ludo.

"Professor Thorpe was breathing. Just. But there were claw marks on his neck, his left arm was almost separated from his shoulder and his legs had been pulverised. It seemed at some point he had brought out an axe, but she had it taken from him. He sat against the wall in the corner of the main room. His eyes were open, but, he was out of it. In front of him, crouched in the corner and giggling, was something that resembled the shape of his wife. She was so far from the pretty young lady, who'd accompanied him that at first they didn't recognise her. Professor Thorpe died before they could get him to the mainland. Which left the thing in the shape of his wife, who never spoke another intelligible word for as long as she gave the impression of life."

"She died in an asylum, didn't she?" I said.

She sighed. "All the money her husband had did finally do good work. It meant she could at least be taken care of her for the rest of her unnatural life. Whenever it ended." She cricked her neck, looking at the island, taking it in. "They were the last people to live here. It's a dreadful old place. You can feel it. So, as I explained to your office, I won't linger long at the dockside. I'll swing around tomorrow and if you're there – if you're in one piece – then I'll return you to the mainland. But otherwise, you'll be on your own."

"Fair enough," Ludo replied.

"I think you'll find the place empty," she said. "I know you say a man has gone there to live, but given its history, I doubt he could live there peaceably. Besides, if he did sneak on in an unknown fashion, I'm sure we'd have heard hints of him by now."

"Oh, I don't think it's a man," Ludo told her.

"That I can believe," she said and gripped the ship's

wheel tighter.

CHAPTER TWENTY-THREE

The dock on the island was old and rotten and obviously unsafe. It had been built from wood and a few metal bolts at the same time the house was constructed in the 1930s. With nearly a hundred years distance, if felt bizarre that – with no one around to perform maintenance – it hadn't been reclaimed by the sea a long time ago. I'll be honest, there was a small hope in my breast, as Angharad pulled her boat alongside it, that she'd misjudge how much space she had and smack into the dock, splintering the whole thing apart. Then we'd have to leave and regroup and find another way to get there.

I'd meant what I said in Botswana. I was with Ludo. But equally, there was a part of me wondering whether all this might be something too big and weird even for us.

Angharad, however, was an expert and brought us in without scraping against the aged wood. Of course there was no one available to tie the boat, even for the moment it would take for us to disembark, so we both had to jump. I went first and on landing skidded on my shoes, but just about held myself upright. Ludo, however, would have dropped flat onto his back if I hadn't caught his arm. We must have made a humorous sight. Two besuited Disney creatures in big yellow raincoats slipping and sliding. But when I looked at her, Angharad hadn't raised a smile.

"Tomorrow morning," she yelled. "I'll come get you if you're around. After that? Well, I'll keep an eye out for you, and if I see you waving from a distance, I'll pop by, but I can't guarantee it."

"Thank you!" I called.

She nodded once. "Try to stay in one piece!" Then she pushed the engine into reverse and backed onto the ocean.

Together we stood and faced the rocks leading up. Directly before the dock, there seemed no feasible path through. Just jagged stone or sheer cliff face.

"If they built a house, there must be a way through to it," said Ludo confidently. Then he jumped onto the shingle and started to walk along the thin stretch of beach. Not caring in the slightest about the wind or the rain, or the surf lapping at his shoes.

"It was funny her mentioning Beddnic, wasn't it?" he said. "This place reminds me of it. But I can't imagine you're going to find the love of your life here."

"I already have the love of my life. I don't need to find another."

"Fair point. I probably won't find the love of my life here either."

I glanced around at the endless grey of sky, sea and rock. "Despite meeting Beryl, what I mostly remember about that night was losing control."

The icy water covered our ankles as we traipsed through the shingle. Soaking us to our shins. Obviously these suits were going to be taken off and never worn again. Possibly they'd need to be burnt. I wondered, with how cold and wet we already were, what tonight might bring. Angharad wasn't going to arrive until morning and so, if nothing else happened, there was a real possibility we'd be frozen before she returned. My teeth chattered and I feared I was on the edge of hyperthermia.

But if Earl Henderson had been truthful with us, and

The Ravens Creature was here, a chill might be the least of our problems.

"How long until sunset do you think?" asked Ludo.

He was the smartest man I knew, could summon forth all kinds of esoteric information in a millisecond's firing of synapses, and yet he gave every indication of not really understanding how the seasons worked.

"With all the clouds and the rain, it feels like the sun hasn't even risen, but I'd say an hour."

He paused casually. An ice cold wave crashed in and soaked his legs right to his thighs, but he pretended not to notice. "Maybe we should have waited until the morning."

"I suggested as much."

"So you did. Do you remember what argument I used against it?"

"You said the bad things were likely to happen here after dark, so there was no point us hanging around in the daylight waiting for them to transpire."

He grinned. "You are completely right there, Garris. Even if I do so hate having my own arguments being used against me, but there you go."

Taking a child's delight in splashing through the water, he turned and marched on. A dread thought occurred that we'd get all the way around the island, but miss the point of egress. We'd wind our way to the dock again, feeling foolish. As we navigated the coast, the rocks seemed to become more dense and unmanageable. Men skilled at this kind of thing who hung grappling hooks off their belts would have considered it twice.

But Ludo started to whistle as he led the way, and (as annoyingly often happened), it turned out he was right. There was eventually a way through.

A path opened across the rocks. It was steep and largely overgrown, but those extra shrubs and foliage gave us something to hang onto. A way to pull ourselves up. In actuality, it was only half a mile from the dock, but it felt we'd travelled much further. Climbing with our wet shoes and cold feet was difficult. The water and the ice weighed them down, but we hauled ourselves across the slope, huffing and grunting.

When we reached the top, we saw it.

I don't know how much volcanic activity there would have been in the land today known as Wales, but I'd be surprised if this island hadn't once been a volcano. In front of us – on the other side of those rocks – was a big, flat, almost perfectly circular field. It was one of the strangest sights I'd ever seen, particularly with the sky so ominous and looming. The grass – waist high – was an incredible shade of green, the like of which I'd never witnessed in nature before. There was a grey blueness to it. A tint which, under this harsh sky, seemed to glimmer. The grass swayed in the wind, every blade moving as one. Bringing to mind an impassable ocean.

And at the heart of it was the house. It was built at the centre of the circle. I couldn't begin to imagine how tortuous the construction project must have been. To bring all the materials to the island, carry them from the dockside around to the one part of the cliffs you can manage to climb, then haul them over, before walking through the strange grass, until you reached the exact middle of this large clear space. I can only hope Professor Thorpe had indeed paid a hell of a lot to have his dream house built.

The circle was so big, we had to be a mile and a half from it, and so couldn't see it as clearly as we would have wanted. Our view was not helped by the fact that the house was grey slate to match the surroundings. A large one-storey affair; wide rather than tall, with a sloped roof. It didn't appear well maintained – I could see green and purple shrubs had taken complete possession of its east facing side wall – but nor did it appear it had been allowed to slide into ruin since the 1930s. The roof was intact, for instance. Clearly, somebody must have been there over the years to look after it, even if only to keep the elements out.

Ludo pointed.

"Do you see what I see, Garris?"

I squinted and I did.

Wisps of smoke coming from the chimney.

With a burst of adrenalin we started forward. We had travelled thousands of miles around the world, but we seemed to have reached our destination.

CHAPTER TWENTY-FOUR

We pushed our way through the grass and tried not to lose our footing on the damp soil.

I'd told Ludo it was an hour until sunset, but the sky seemed almost unbelievably distant when we were in the basin of this island. In Botswana, the firmament had been phenomenally vast, but here it seemed the sky belonged to another place. What was above us was merely a representation of sky. It wouldn't matter when the sun set, this island would bring on the darkness sooner.

On the boat, I had imagined a mansion. But it was even smaller than it looked from the ridge. One of the rare occasions where a house becomes less impressive the closer you came to it. Some of the windows were broken, cladding had been lost off most of the walls, while a good portion of the roof tiles were loose.

Yet, through one of the windows to the left of the front door, there seemed to be the faint gleam of candlelight.

It seemed the thing which had once been Jacob Ravens was at home.

I wondered if he – or it – was in there watching us. It can hardly have missed our approach in our bright yellow garb. There was no movement anywhere else on the island.

159

No birds seemed to land on this wide grey expanse. Probably the thing would have heard the engine of Angharad's boat, and known somebody was on their way. Now it would see us, on the one route we could take, hurrying across the grass.

Ludo, despite being a head height shorter than me, could whip up a pace when he wanted to. There were points when he got ahead of me. In fact, on the last stretch, when the ground beneath our feet felt harder – even if the grass lost none of its uniform length – he located an extra gear and arrived at the front door first.

I don't know how he felt, but with the exertion, I was sweating under the raincoat. My suit adding to its collection of stains.

I pulled up and walked the last few yards. There was no point both of us getting there at a run. I glanced at the window to the left of the front door. It was gloomy and dark. There didn't seem to be any light escaping anymore. Had the occupant snuffed the candle, or had I imagined it?

With a glance at me, Ludo grabbed an old silver knocker and hit it three times. The sound echoed, going beyond the house and reverberating around the basin of the island. We stood and regarded the door. It was heavy wood and had once been painted black. Although where it hadn't flaked away completely, the colour had faded more to grey. Evidently it had been replaced at some point in the last hundred years. As exposed to the elements as it was, the original door would have rotted to nothing a long time ago.

There's a peculiar silence which comes from a door which isn't opening. Normally you imagine it's the echo of the empty house, but this one had it with smoke coming from the chimney and candlelight recently in the window. What greeted us then was an uninviting sound; a deliberate absence of noise which says *go away and try another day*. It was the sound of being ignored. Most people would creep back through the grass and take the house's suggestion, but quitting and plodding towards the dock wasn't an option for us this day.

And whoever was inside would have known that.

Ludo raised the knocker and banged once more, with the same result.

The two of us simply stood there.

"A shame," he said. "After everything we've gone through the last couple of days, I rather thought we'd have the red carpet, champagne and canapes."

He moved from the door and went to the window which had recently flickered with candle light. Actually placing his nose to the glass and peering in.

"Garris," he said. "I think there's a body sprawled across the floor in there."

CHAPTER TWENTY-FIVE

It took me until the third attempt of throwing my weight against the door to force it open. Each time my frame bounced from it. Then the hinges flew apart, sending shrapnel of wood flying. The door swung open, intact. Another sign this place had had more visitors than Angharad had supposed: there'd been a new lock placed on the front door.

It was the smell which hit us first. Musty. But it wasn't merely age and decay which assaulted our nostrils, there was something else to it. A quality which seemed almost alive, which seeped towards us. A sentient gas, perhaps? I thought for a second the house was exhaling. It was letting go its long-stored breath. Which meant, when we went through the door, we'd be stepping into a living creature. The floor would be soft like a tongue, while the walls would be made of flesh. We wouldn't be walking into a house; we'd be willingly climbing into a set of jaws and venturing into its intestines.

Inside was all gloom, and we stood motionless in the doorway trying to pierce it. To see clearly enough we could get a glimpse of what was ahead. Surely neither of us genuinely believed the house was alive. That – despite breaking through the door — the second we stepped through, a mouth would close and seal us up forever. But we both hung back. Wary, ponderous and quickly retrieving our standard issue torches — in case our worst fears were realised.

Torchlight revealed the interior to be merely an old and battered hallway. It was almost disappointing to see after my fears had scarpered away with themselves. The walls and floor were not made of flesh. There were no teeth waiting to sink down upon us. No gullet anxious to swallow our bodies whole. Instead there was a hallway which was old and neglected. The walls, as one would expect after this amount of time, were bare. There were a few scraps of a faded floral wallpaper hanging at odd corners, but the rest had either been torn off, or else seen its glue fail and tumbled itself free. The floorboards were bare, but appeared solid enough. Standing on them shouldn't plummet us feet-first into the basement. There was no other furniture, and there was no hint of any light-source. Nor any sense of heat from a fire. We'd not be drying off our suits any time soon. Now we were inside the hallway, it was pretending to be a deserted house, and not doing a poor job.

"This way!" urged Ludo.

He stepped through, moving tentatively along the corridor. I guess that while his eyes had seen how solid the floorboards were, an innate sense of self-preservation didn't truly believe it. Hence his caution. The door leading to the left side of the house was closed, and Ludo moved cautiously towards it. The boards creaked underneath his tread and announced our approach. I walked directly behind him. While he kept his beam steady and looked ahead at where he was going, I shone mine around, trying to see if there was anything we might have missed.

There was nothing so far. It was a decrepit old hallway. I kept telling myself it was only a decrepit old hallway in a decrepit old house.

Ludo reached out a hand and pushed open the door to

the room we had seen through the window.

For a second, it appeared there was a light in there. That the candle we'd seen when running had been freshly relit. But, without there seeming to be any movement in the room at all, it disappeared. Ludo and I blinked, unsure whether we had really seen it, or if it had been a flickering mirage of illumination.

Guided only by torchlight, we stepped together through the doorway.

There was no body stretched out in the centre of the room. Ludo had been mistaken on that. But there was the skin of a polar bear laid across the stone floor. Its head propped up, so it seemed to be roaring with fury. Elsewhere were the taxidermy carcasses of a brown bear, and in the opposite corner a lion. Both posed with lifelike ferocity. Around the room were the heads of a panther, a wolf and an alligator. Each of them mounted snarling on the bare brick wall. There was also more than one anaconda. Their jaws separated, as if ready to swallow a man. It was like the drawing-room in Earl Henderson's now burned home taken to excess. A parody of it. But whereas in Botswana, all of those trophies had the air of misplaced triumph, these all simply screamed *death*.

The true pièce de résistance was fixed above the fireplace. I shuddered as my gaze reached it. It was a werewolf in mid-transformation: the face of the wolf tearing its way free of the face of the man. So we could see the teeth and the dark hunger in its yellow eyes, but also the fearful glance of the man losing himself. My experience was that if you shot a werewolf, the beast vanished, and the body returned to human form. So I had no idea how this corpse could have been achieved, but I didn't doubt for a second the veracity of it.

Ludo shone his torch in its direction. "Interesting," he said without emotion. "If I had to guess, I'd say this was a purchase from the Earl Henderson boutique. All of these animals seemed to have been arranged for a purpose, and

I'm guessing this one is the crucial element of it all."

"What the hell is this place?" I asked.

"I don't know. But it's quite the collection, isn't it? Even to us, it feels distinctly eerie."

"Definitely."

"I doubt even the most ardent animal rights' groups would want to spend too long in here pouring red paint over them."

We shone the torches around. Their beams trying to hunt for a pattern we weren't yet seeing.

But then the door to the room slammed shut.

We jumped, but fortunately didn't drop our torches.

However, before we could reassure ourselves it was the wind and nothing truly bad was happening, every creature in the room — be they severed head or posed carcass — suddenly gained an unnatural light in their eyes and growled or hissing at us.

CHAPTER TWENTY-SIX

Together we leapt towards the same spot near the window. Behind the polar bear, but hopefully not so close to the werewolf it could swing out a claw and grab us. We'd moved away from the door. But neither of us believed – now it had slammed shut – that it would be unlocked. We stood with our backs to each other, our torches outstretched as if weapons, and tried not to yell in panic.

For a moment there was a cacophony of animal outrage, but then the growls of the beasts subsided and their eyes returned to deadness. Nothing moved. In actuality, nothing had moved at all. Despite the noise, those creatures hadn't hauled themselves free from their deaths and launched themselves towards us. It could have been that we'd hallucinated that brief burst of furious life. Ludo and I stood pressed together, torches hunting for any actual movement, but our breathing returned somewhat to normal.

"A nice parlour trick!" Ludo called. He stepped from me, his eyes scanning around the room, seeking someone to address with his compliments. "Although a little clichéd. I suppose when you were alive, you were a bit of a hack, weren't you? I'm not going to expect too much from you here then. But for what it was, it was very effective. I enjoyed it massively. You appreciated it too, didn't you, Garris?"

I nodded as enthusiastically as I could.

"How's it done?" asked Ludo. "I realise you stage conjurers don't want to reveal the secrets of your craft, but it's only us here, and I promise Garris and I won't tell. Well, Garris certainly won't. I can be overly talkative, but I cross my chest and hope for indigestion. The eyes were easy enough to do, I'm guessing. They all have miniature bulbs in them, don't they? You can remotely switch them on and off. The same is true of the roaring, isn't it? You have a digital file containing those sounds and you have little speakers hidden right across the room to make us think the noise was coming from all around us."

He stepped forward, smiling and trying to radiate bravado.

"What next?" he said. "Are you going to drop a smoke bomb and emerge in front of us wearing a Dracula cape and a smug grin? We'll give you a round of applause if you do. Encouragement to get you on with the rest of your act. All the time hoping you'll have something which actually impresses us. I'm quite small, so my proportions won't really work if you want to put me in a box and saw me in half. Garris might be up for it though. Do you have any doves you're going to pull from hats? How about close-up magic with a deck of cards? *That* I like. It's properly impressive. Can you do something similar for us, or are you more geared towards the big and tacky illusion?"

But there was nothing. No response. He was trying to goad our host, but getting zero reaction. Nevertheless I emulated him and tried to put as much casualness into my stance as I could. Willing my hand steady when I noticed the pumping adrenalin made my torch beam shake. If I'm honest, I wasn't convinced Ludo's strategy was the correct one. We both knew what had happened with those dead animals wasn't simple trickery and sleight-of-hand. It had been the real thing. With that in mind, did we really want to see what could be done as an encore? It sure as hell wasn't going to be card tricks.

A minute must have moved past when we stood there waiting for something to happen. For there to be a second act. For our host, wherever he might be, to make the next move.

Ludo shrugged and stepped forward to look at the walls. Standing tantalisingly close to the animal heads.

"Come on!" Ludo said, although his tone wasn't quite as antagonistic now. "We're waiting. We haven't paid for tickets for this show, but we bought some for the boat, so we deserve entertainment after our trip. What have you got for us? I've never been overly fond of rabbits. I can't say why. They've never seemed as cute to me as they do to pretty much everyone else. So if you're planning to pull one from a top hat, be warned that you're only going to get polite applause from my direction..." He tapered off. Whatever this Ravens Creature was, wherever it was, it apparently wasn't going to bite and react to Ludo's condescension.

Beside the door was an old-fashioned desk bureau, and there were a couple of armchairs in the corners of the room. But they weren't what caught my attention as I swung the beam. I realised there were animals I'd missed on my first sweep. A coyote, a huge fox, various birds of prey, more big cats. All of which were utterly still, but capable of bursting into a version of life at any second.

At least the ones Earl Henderson had mounted around his room were sedate.

Careful not to get too close to any of the dead animals. My eyes caught by various symbols carved into the naked brick. Words and hieroglyphs and archaic runes. Dead languages from long ago.

Ludo shone his torch at these carvings as well.

"Do you recognise them?" he asked.

"It's similar to the symbols on the casket in

Killamurray."

"Yes, when the Picasso Twins used a Jacob Ravens story to create a ghost machine. I think this illustration is particularly familiar."

My eye settled on something I absolutely recognised. A depiction of mythical beasts, including dragons, griffins and sea serpents. As well as real-life hunters like lions, bears and snakes. All of them represented with their teeth and claws at their sharpest. They were apex hunters, but they were peering upwards. They were both cowering before something and worshipping it. In Ireland, however, the 'it' in question wasn't shown. But here it was.

A giant raven.

"Look!" My voice emerged as a whisper.

He nodded. "I see it. When this place was built, Jacob Ravens was only at the start of his career. But evidently there were some who were expecting great things from him." His fingers ran over symbols in a language I had never seen before. "This looks familiar too."

"From where?" I asked.

"Arthur Haberdash's scribblings."

Haberdash had been a mentor of sorts to Jacob Ravens, until – so the story went – the pair had a massive falling-out. But apparently he had also been the man who spoke the midnight incantation at Ravens's fake funeral in England.

"You haven't read much Jacob Ravens, but you have read Arthur Haberdash? He's much more obscure these days."

"I haven't read his pulp horror," Ludo explained. "But after Killamurray, and a few other things, I decided I needed to do additional research. So I have read Haberdash's *Glossary of Other Worlds*. Well, skimmed it, actually. Rumour had it that, like Ravens, Haberdash went to these other worlds. But he found himself trapped in a whole other dominion and had to fight for his life to escape."

"It was Ravens who abandoned him in the other realm, wasn't it?"

Ludo nodded. "But on his return – or his supposed return – Haberdash wrote what he called the glossary, which was part dictionary and part almanac of these strange places. It doesn't hang together well. Some descriptions are much better and more evocative than others. But in the appendix of incantations, I swear he includes this exact sequence of symbols."

"You can't actually interpret it, can you?"

"No. There's so much I don't know, Garris. Lots lost in the shadows, and *that* makes me anxious. We're here. We've come and, whilst I didn't expect a welcoming committee, I did anticipate a welcome. But…" He turned from the writing on the wall. "It's the same thing right the way through this affair, isn't it? Hints of something beyond, and warnings of the ominous, but nothing to tell us what we're dealing with. I have a feeling that this might, unfortunately, be all steam and reflective surfaces."

I can't remember what I was going to say next, I probably had words of encouragement to offer, but whatever they were, they caught in my throat.

Instead another sound came, a croaky rustle which was barely a human voice at all: "I'm sorry it hasn't lived up to your expectations, gentlemen. *As yet.*"

CHAPTER TWENTY-SEVEN

We both jumped. The voice striking us, so sudden and unexpected and strange.

It had come from the corner nearest the window. Where one of the armchairs stood. There was something there we'd missed. *Someone* there we'd missed. I tried to calm my heart, which was attempting to escape through my throat, and shone the torch across to it. We'd been so engrossed with the animals and those runes on the walls, that what should have been obvious eluded us. There was another person in there with us.

Trying to hold the torch steady, I sent the beam in the direction of the speaker.

On the wall next to the chair was the head of a snake. Its features elongated, so it appeared ready to destroy its prey. Sharp fangs gleamed in the light. I had taken in this particular work of taxidermy already. But my beam moved down to the old and battered armchair below it. The chair was red leather, and I'd somehow already noted that the arms were worn to the wood. But I hadn't spotted that the pile of rags I thought had been dumped in the seat wasn't a pile of rags at all. There was something moving within them.

Ludo's torch-beam joined mine. Shoulder to shoulder,

we shone the light and interrogated those rags. There were a few seconds when I thought I was mistaken. They were old cloths, after all. There was a flicker of relief on my part. I'd convinced myself I was finally going to see The Ravens Creature, but I was only looking at scraps of material. Grey, aged and surely on the verge of disintegrating.

But then there was the faintest shifting within the chair.

A person desperate to cling onto the rational order of things would undoubtedly have tried to claim the movement was caused by wind. That this was only cloth, and it had been disturbed by a breeze Ludo and I couldn't feel.

It was at that moment the eyes shone outwards.

Within the cloth, reflecting our torches back at us, were two narrow slits. I stared at them and slowly determined the dark contours of a face. The head was human, but the eyes were those of a ravenous feline. Yellow, with a thick black vertical line of a pupil. These eyes peered unblinking directly into our light-beams.

The animals around us didn't growl this time; they started to scream.

Every one of them on the walls, and on the floor, let out a cry of absolute fear. The sound swamped the room, a choir of torture from each corner. It was as if every one of these already deceased creatures was reliving their death throes. As if whatever agony they'd experienced towards the end came back to them. More intense and unendurable, as they knew there was no escape. It was unceasing. The first time they felt this pain, they may have clung onto hope, convinced themselves they could possibly get away. Or grasped at the knowledge that this was the end of any feeling. But experiencing the pain once more when their heads were mounted on the walls, or their carcass had been skinned and dumped to the floor, extinguished any glimmer of hope. There was only death on top of death, and the cries at that knowledge were excruciating.

The worst sound came from the werewolf. Both man

and beast managed to scream at once. Undoubtedly the man had been screaming for a long time, his soul caught in this dreadful place from which he couldn't escape. But it was the beast's cry which was harsher. Its taste of triumph destroyed. Its embryonic body caught forever, not quite free of its original weaker form. There was only one mouth, but there were two creatures there, and the two of them were never going to escape each other or the agonies they had to endure.

Ludo and I couldn't help ourselves. At The Organisation we'd had training on how to face up to all kinds of bizarre events, but primal fear can be overwhelming. We both took backwards steps towards the shut door. Doing our best not to tread on the polar bear. Not knowing where else we could go, but desperate to get away.

How long it lasted, I can't guess. But it stopped in an instant. The noise, which had been utterly oppressive, vanished into the air without an echo.

Ludo and I stood there breathless, trying to put ourselves together again. Our torchlight pointed in the vague direction of the rags, but not with any zeal.

Gradually, as I stopped hearing my heartbeat rushing through my ears, I realised the agonised wails hadn't given way to complete silence. No, there was chuckling in its wake. A low and unpleasant wheeze of laughter in the same cracked voice which had spoken to us.

Ludo straightened, raised his torch to the side of his head and took a step closer. What he found in the armchair was no longer going to be mistaken for old cloth. It was obviously a man. Or something in the shape of a man. The skin of its face was a greyish brown, unlike any human I'd ever seen. It was drawn so tight to its skull, that at points it seemed to have cracked to allow glimpses of the bone underneath. There was no nose, no eyelids and no lips. It regarded us with those yellow eyes, and a thin snake-like tongue glided across its lower jaw.

"Merely a little parlour trick of mine," it said, the voice a croak, but with the timbre of education. There was a well-bred Englishness to it, even as it barely sounded like a man. "A performance we hackneyed magicians do. But far better than card tricks, wouldn't you agree?"

The room started to become brighter. A lime green glow began to fill the air, illuminating the room in a sickly shade of light and rendering our torches superfluous.

It was hard to tear my eyes from this being in the corner, but I think I was aware the runes in the wall had started to glow. Everything else shone sickly green, but those words were bright red.

Then the creature lurched forward in the chair, its face looming. "Are you not ready for me?" it rasped. "Let me introduce myself. *I am your monster!*"

CHAPTER TWENTY-EIGHT

I felt ice at my spine and realised the temperature in the room had plummeted. It was as if my sweat was freezing on exposure to the air. The creature stared at us and we held its gaze. Without having moved, its face seemed to fill my vision, but I was unable to determine much shape beneath those robes. I thought it would be man-like, that there would be a torso with arms and legs, but it was impossible to tell. There was just dark cloth and the strange skull of a face, and the malignancy of its eyes.

In reality, probably only a minute had passed since it had revealed himself, yet it seemed much longer. I stood on the spot paralysed. Near enough to the door that I might have leapt for it, but knowing that trying the handle would be useless. There was no way this thing was going to let us walk away. We were sealed in.

Ludo regained his poise much quicker than I. He straightened himself, but so languidly he could have been going for a stretch and a yawn, then he switched off his torch. Neat and unflustered, he lifted the raincoat and opened his jacket and tucked it into his inside pocket. Then he smoothed the layers down again and stood and regarded the creature with his hands crossed in front of him. An odd look of expectation resided on his face.

"Would I be correct in thinking," he said, in his plumiest tones, "that you are Jacob Ravens?"

The creature narrowed its eyes, perhaps surprised by Ludo's sang-froid as well. But then it emitted a long hiss. Not words this time, instead a snarl of annoyance and aggression.

"Or you would prefer not to answer to the name?" said Ludo. "Do you not like the moniker? Is it not one you would own to? If so, I think I can understand your rationale. It's a long time since you were *him*, so I can see why you would want to create a little distance. But," he said, as he trailed one foot along the floor while his gaze moved across the various carcasses on the walls, "I'm not sure changing your name to 'our monster' is necessarily the best way forward. It lacks a certain friendliness. It becomes its own self-fulfilling prophecy. As you claim you are our monster, but it needn't necessarily be the case. You're aware of that, aren't you?"

"Are you going to lecture me on what I am?" The creature's voice was gravelly, but matched Ludo's in poshness.

"Oh, I appreciate where you come from. You are born from the soul of a tremendously dangerous man and have spent your formative years locked in a coffin. It's not the kind of background which would make you a natural optimist. You're almost a creature from a fairy tale. But now you're out, and you're with us, a monster isn't necessarily what you have to be."

I think I went to say something, to echo Ludo's comments. But my mouth wouldn't open to produce any sounds. I blinked and tried to understand what was happening; and as I did, the green light swam in front of me, while the red markings on the walls became brighter.

The realisation came that I couldn't move.

"What am I then?" it asked. "If I am not a monster, how will you treat me?"

"What do you mean?"

It chuckled. "Will you welcome me into your family homes? Will you offer me respect? Or will you lock me away for examination in your London headquarters and run experiments on me? This *non*-monster you travelled halfway around the world for."

Ludo stepped forward, a smile rising to his lips. "How do you know me, by the way? Why have you gone to all this effort to call me towards you?"

With all my strength, I tried to open my mouth and yell. But nothing came.

"I see the world differently to you," the creature snarled. "I understand you differently to how you understand yourselves."

"Given what we do," said Ludo, "Garris and I see the world differently to most people too. It's an occupational hazard. But it doesn't mean I can zero in on particular individuals and assign importance to them, as you seem to have done with me."

He glanced in my direction, and a crease of worry reached his forehead at my lack of movement. I tried to signal with my eyes that I was frozen.

"Don't be modest," said the creature. "In the half-world I occupy, you must realise your name crops up. It is mentioned. I have ascertained all sorts of things about the both of you. I have had time to research into you. You and Garris."

Hearing it drag my name in a tone almost guttural was a cold knife across my belly.

"Are you okay there, Garris?" asked Ludo casually.

But I didn't answer. I couldn't answer.

Instead the creature spoke:

"I have had help along the way, of course, but so have you. Help from people who brought you exactly where I wanted you to be, right in front of me."

It released a long hiss of sulphur. If it had been louder and more projected, it might have been a scream, but it was like gas escaping into the room. It blended with the green glow.

"We know you brought us here." I could see that Ludo was focusing on the thing in the chair, while trying not to let any worry for me show. "And of course we realised it was a trap. It was incredibly obvious. But what we couldn't determine, without properly meeting you, is why you wanted *us*. What all this is in aid of. So we came here. We walked into your trap. So we could speak to you and learn what you're up to." He brushed invisible lint from the front of his jacket. "What do I call you, by the way? Would Jacob Ravens suffice? Or is there another name the new you would prefer?"

In nearly every scrape we ever found ourselves, I always admired Ludo's unruffled assurance. How he could unleash impeccable politeness – with a hint of aloofness – in the direst situations. Normally I tried to support him. To chip in a remark or two where I could. Now, however, I couldn't speak. My mouth refused to open. It was exceedingly dry. Nor could I reliably move any other muscle. I was trapped a couple of feet from the door. A human statue; not too dissimilar to those stuffed animals. I peered through the window and realised how black the sky was. The clouds had hung heavy when it was daylight, now they lingered and ensured no glow from the moon penetrated through.

Before us, the creature blinked its yellow eyes slowly at Ludo, and snarled: "Do you think I would own to *that* name?"

"Why not?" asked Ludo reasonably. "With a little distance, have you decided you don't like his writings? Or are you embarrassed to have fallen so far out of popularity? Or given how vain a man you allegedly were, do you not like being seen in rags and badly in need of moisturiser?" He grinned. "The Ravens Creature is how Earl Henderson described you: is that one better?"

The creature wheezed a chuckle.

"What have you done to Garris, by the way?" Ludo

seemed ready to take a step towards me, but then thought better of it. Perhaps he feared it might make things worse. "Is this another of your parlour tricks? If so, then this time I *am* impressed. But you need to put a stop to it. You have made your point."

"Parlour trick?" The creature scoffed. "You have no comprehension of what I'm capable of doing."

Ludo shot a glance in my direction, his pallor pale under the green light, but then he set his jaw firm. "Illuminate me!"

Rain hammered against the roof. It had eased since the storm on the boat, but in an instant it exploded above us. There should have been nothing unusual in this. We were at one of the most westward points of Wales. Rain was no surprise in whatever form it came. But the storm arrived with ominous timing.

"That wasn't you, was it?" Ludo smiled. He covered any nerves by slicking his hand through his hair. "Okay, *that* was impressive. Do you have anything else? Stopping Garris moving is one thing, and I would be grateful to you for halting whatever spell you've put him under before we continue this conversation further. What is the point of what you've done to him, after all? Why have you done it?"

"You want to understand, do you?" it growled.

"Yes!" said Ludo. "Of course I want to understand. What is it you want? Why are you here? When are you going to let Garris go?"

It was subtler than previously – unaccompanied by roaring – but I felt every animal in the room fix its eyes on Ludo. I don't know if he felt it as well, such was his focus on the creature in the rags, but Ludo was facing a wider audience.

"I owe you no explanations," The Ravens Creature said. "There is no way you can understand all which is within me. Do you have any idea of the way I see the world?"

"Amaze me!" Ludo barked.

"I am far beyond your plane of existence. I created myself, and in doing so became more than you. You hear of creatures of myth and creatures out of time, and I am both and much more. I have seen worlds and realities you could not apprehend."

Ludo spoke across the creature. "You've spent the last seventy years locked in a box. Let's not get too carried away with your 'what I did on my summer holidays' essay."

The rain lashed against the window behind the creature. Coming in so strong it rattled the frames.

"These experiences you talk of," said Ludo, "are you sure they're real? You have the mind of a horror writer inside you. A fantasy author. And not a good one. These things you hail as memories, what makes you so positive they happened? Can you guarantee they're real? You are the remains of Jacob Ravens, and Jacob Ravens had an overactive imagination, so there's a good chance you're making up all this stuff. His writing is all pan-dimensional goblins and ghouls, isn't it?"

The creature laughed. It took me a few seconds to recognise the sound. At first, there was a flicker of hope that it might be choking. Its throat closing. But no, it was laughter. A deep hacking sound which could have been mistaken for a thousand insects mating.

"You have not fully read the author, Ravens?" it asked at last.

"Can you see that in my head?" asked Ludo. "Interesting. I've skimmed through. Explored the odd corner here and there. But a proper deep dive? Well, I've never had the time or the inclination." He gave his fullest grin. "Is it worth it? All I hear are bad things. That saying about how no author is unjustifiably remembered? Well, my perception is Jacob Ravens – or *you*, if you won't give us any other name – is justifiably forgotten. Completely and utterly so. The preserve these days of weirdos and cranks. Those desperate shut-ins who pore over his work because it takes them from their own lonely realities." He took a step towards me. "This conversation will be a lot easier for me if Garris was by my side and able to chip in."

The creature rocked a little in its chair. "You have not properly read Jacob Ravens? It surprises me. I did not expect that at all."

"If you really wanted someone who has explored your work, couldn't you have found a fan-club list to go through?" Ludo suggested. "Surely such a thing wouldn't have taken too long."

But The Ravens Creature ignored him, diverting his gaze at last in my direction, letting those ugly eyes scrape over me. "What of your quiet friend?" He sniffed. "I see he has read more than you. In other circumstances, he would do as a back-up."

"Back-up?" asked Ludo.

I tried to open my mouth, to speak for myself, but of course nothing came.

The creature laughed, this time a fuller and huskier sound – a laugh which was also a declaration of warfare.

Wind and rain smashed the windows; while inside the various animal carcasses were regarding the two of us hungrily. The runes on the wall were not only glowing, they had started to burn. It was like they were heating up in the brick, scorching their way through it.

For a few seconds, I thought I was imagining it. But then I saw Ludo shudder. He turned and stared all the way around the room, as if to make sure they were burning throughout. I couldn't look myself – I couldn't do anything – but I could tell from his face they were.

"Okay, let's stop dancing around." Ludo stared at the armchair. "What's happening?"

"Whilst I would have preferred you to have the vast majority of Ravens in your mind," drawled the creature. "You were always my secondary vessel. Garris was far more important to my purposes."

"Garris!" he gasped. "Why?"

"I left the clues for you, as I understood you would not be able to resist them. I knew you would track them across the world. But it was Michael Garris I truly sought. And I also knew he would be by your side."

Ludo's jaws clenched. "Tell me what's happening to him. Why do you want him?"

The creature chuckled: "Have you never asked yourself where the wolf in his mind came from? Lots of people encounter werewolves. They are almost commonplace if you know where to look. But they can usually only infect with their bite. So how did this one manage to get into his head? How does it stay there?"

"I don't know. Tell me how!" yelled Ludo. Any calmness completely gone.

"Because the wolf he met was from another realm. One beyond ours. And Garris's encounter with it opened a chink between our world and the wolf's natural home. The smallest fissure in your friend's mind which I am going to force open."

"What?"

"The words you recognised from old Haberdash's so-called work are '*I am the gate to beyond and I shall open*'. And your friend," it paused and then laughed, "Garris is living proof that those words retain their power. *He* is the gate to beyond! The circle is complete. I am going to blow him apart and then blow this world apart."

CHAPTER TWENTY-NINE

Ludo grabbed my arm and shook it frantically. His fingers pressing into the sleeves of my jacket and twisting, wringing the material. I could feel him leaving bruises on my biceps, but I didn't respond. I didn't move at all. He could have grabbed a block of wood and smashed it against my ribcage and I wouldn't have reacted. Admittedly, the momentum of the blow would have knocked me over, but nothing would have happened from my initiative.

"Garris!" he bawled. "You can fight this. Whatever it is, you can beat it." He let go of my arm and turned towards The Ravens Creature, but of course couldn't offer a pretence of calmness anymore. "What on earth is this?"

"It is the reason you are here," The Ravens Creature grated coldly.

It had raised itself from the armchair, but I wasn't sure it was standing. The rags it wore fell like robes and shrouded around its feet. It could have been my panicked mind projecting, but I thought the thing was levitating.

In the far reaches of my mind, I heard a hungry wolf howl.

"You've brought us here to kill Garris?"

"I needed an open mind. The average person's is far too closed. Their comprehension too limited. I needed a mind that could imagine some things which exist beyond. I needed a person who had touched other worlds. The information came to me – through circuitous routes – about the wolf in your friend's head, and I understood what it meant. I realised it would allow me to open the gateway I needed. The circle is complete."

"What circle? A gateway to where?"

"Oh, you are sneering. Your quant assertion that the things in my head might be fantasy, that I had imagined them, or inherited someone else's delusions. How pathetic. How pitiful. No," the voice said sternly, "it is all *very* real! There are other realms out there, and they are going to pour into here tonight. Through your friend's head."

"But I didn't read any of your books. Isn't that important anymore?"

The creature sighed. "It would only have been important if your friend didn't make it. If he'd died in transit. But he is here, and the wolf in his mind is hungry for escape."

Ludo gazed at the wolf combined with the man on the wall.

"That's why you got this item from Earl Henderson, isn't it? All these carnivores are here to excite the animal in Garris's mind. But that one is the most important of all. An actual visualisation to the wolf of what it's like to be trapped in a man."

I felt my muscles hardening, becoming calcified. I tried to move. With every ounce of willpower I attempted to force myself into movement, but nothing happened. I was trapped and paralysed. A dumb witness to my annihilation.

Beside me, Ludo was becoming more desperate. "Say I believe you, what exactly is going to come through here?"

"Oh," it answered. "I assure you, it will be interesting! A thousand creatures beyond your imaginings. Races of men who do not obey your constructs and will take this world from you. Along with a million breeds of carnivore which will enjoy devouring your soft flesh. The author Ravens thought this was far too cosy a reality, and that is why he went elsewhere. I have to agree with the long-ago man. Only I am going to bring the elsewhere to here."

"Let me guess, there will not only be werewolves, but lions with wings which can breathe fire?"

It gave a horrifying chuckle. "It is the least of what is possible. The man who calls himself Earl Henderson may see himself as a skilled hunter, but he is too timid to go further than the edges. I am going to bring all of it through and meld these other worlds with this one."

"But why?" screamed Ludo. "What for? Why would you do this? What do you get out of it?"

"Because elsewhere is where I belong. Look at me! Properly stare. Tell me what kind of life I would lead if I was here, with nothing at all from my reality. I would be made a prisoner and a test subject. If I stay here and do nothing, then I will only be your monster. But this way, I shall become a god."

"Your vanity is poking through there, Ravens," Ludo said. "But why not simply go there? Why bring it here? You surely don't need Garris for you alone to make the journey. The original you didn't."

A sneer creased its features. "Because man created me here. I didn't want to be here, I didn't want to exist at all, but man created me here. And so bringing this through is the least I can do to return the favour."

The howling got closer. Ringing in my ears. There was a pressure building in my head. A swelling and unbearable pain. If I'd been able to move, I would have shaken my head, or blown my nose and tried to alleviate it. But as it was, I could do nothing. Except hurt inwardly, excruciatingly.

Ludo turned to me and then to The Ravens Creature. I think he went for a dismissive laugh, but such was the swirl of emotions it emerged cruel.

"And what happens to you? I guess if you're making this

hole in realities, but don't do it right, you could end up toppling into Lord knows where. But what happens if you succeed? What will become of you when these wild beasts burst through? Do you think these carnivores are going to look at you and see something to worship? No, they're going to consider you an apéritif. You're not a main course. At most, you're one bite of a snack and then they'll rampage past you."

The wolf was in my mind. It had existed at the edge for a long time, but tonight it was taking control. It had hidden away from the strange lion, yet now its courage was rejuvenated. Already I could sense the terrible beasts approaching, but the wolf didn't quail. Maybe it was the proximity of The Ravens Creature. Perhaps my inner werewolf concluded that if it was close enough to the source of power, it would gain an advantage.

"You will be the first one eaten," countered The Ravens Creature. It moved over the floor to Ludo, most definitely floating. "For all your gifts of language, you will be no more than the first mouthful. Your friend will be blown apart, and you will be dead in seconds. But for now, I need you to be quiet."

Its finger stretched, expanding, so it extended to nearly three feet long, and pressed onto Ludo's forehead.

The pressure within my head was unbearable. It had reached the top of my skull and there was nowhere else for it to go. The wolf was consuming me from within. I could barely hear or see or think. My jaw dropped open, and at last I expressed something.

I howled.

CHAPTER THIRTY

It felt like both my soul and body were being torn apart. The wolf's claws reaching from within and slicing me open. I would fall into two sundered segments, and the lycanthrope would be left standing in my place. Its fur dripping with my blood and innards.

I could see it. The wolf I had carried for so long was clear to me. This beast was much stronger and more venerable than the creature I'd encountered in Scotland. It stood upright; its spine straight like a man's. Its pelt was silver and glowed under the moonlight, while its red eyes were burning with rage. Its incisors were as sharp as scimitars, and almost too large to fit into its mouth. The beast howled at me. It howled through me.

But it wasn't alone.

Behind it was a monster huge and hideous. A crab creature with one heavy claw pushed in front of it like the gun on a tank. This creature possessed a solitary white eye, which made up the only piece of soft flesh I could see below its iron-hard carapace. The eye was surrounded by thick dark brown hair, which had parasites as big as human hands crawling through it. Its shell was red and battle-scarred. It was bigger than the average house and I imagined it could demolish pretty much everything in its path.

Once the wolf tore its way through my body, this crab was going to follow through and rampage across the world.

There was nothing I could do to prevent any of this. I couldn't move. My mouth hung open. I screamed. Or at least I thought I screamed. It was the sound I heard in my head, but from my mouth there emerged a howl. The wolf used my mouth to howl at the night sky and the far distant moon – furious and hungry – while my face revealed how terrified I was.

Beside me, Ludo too had frozen. The Ravens Creature's elongated, skeletal finger seemed to hold him as paralysed as me. Neither of us could move.

The Ravens Creature floated in front of us, huge now. In this reality it filled my vision, but there were so many other realities I could see. One laid on top of another.

From a different world, I witnessed ten thousand skittering and nibbling creatures coming towards me. They were bugs. Black, with screwed-up faces and incisors. They had no eyes and seemed to feel by touch and ate everything which got in their way. Literally everything. Nightmarish locusts. There was nothing, no matter how tough or durable they couldn't consume. Each had the proportions of a family car. Lined up next to each other, their number must have been ten miles wide and stretched to a sickly green horizon. The knowledge came to me that kings with names I cannot pronounce, on lands I couldn't conceive of, had used these bugs to remove whole cities from their maps. They'd simply pointed them in the right direction and set them rampaging. They were coming straight towards me. They were going to force themselves into this remote corner of Wales and spill into our world.

The brief gap of water between us and the rest of Britain wasn't going to matter to them, any more than it did to the crab creature. They'd clog the channel with the sheer number of their bodies.

Again I tried to turn the sound coming from between

my lips into a scream, if only to relieve the intense pressure my roiling brain was under. In my entire life, I'd never felt such fear. I'd never experienced this level of helplessness. The wolf was filling me. It was taking away everything which was me. It was going to tear my insides apart.

There was another scream. I thought for an instant it was Ludo, but a quick dart from the corner of my eyes told me his mouth remained closed. Even though agony showed on his face. No, it was The Ravens Creature which was screaming. But not in pain; it was articulating joy and anticipation. A raspy cry of triumph.

I saw a sounder of pigs, but they were unlike any pigs I had ever seen. Their skin was an almost luminous shade of pink, and incredibly greasy. A lard-like substance dripped from them with every movement. Their bodies were huge, but their heads were almost the same size. It should have been impossible for them to move, but they ambled along together. Small feral eyes always scanning what was around them. Each had a thatch of bright straw-coloured scraggly fur at the top of its head, like an unkempt bowl of hair. They also had thick, constantly rigid phalluses swinging between their hind legs. These pig beasts snorted and snarled at each other. But a human being seeing one (rather than the whole sounder) for the first time might have thought it was friendly. He could have leant across to pat its head, as he might have done with a real pig. But if so, he'd have lost his hand and then everything else to slavering and crushing jaws. These things were remorseless. They would tear apart and destroy everything which crossed their path. I knew instinctively it was their nature.

They were from a different world to the wolf, but were massing behind it. I could see one of those pig creatures staring at the wolf. Its narrow black eyes also taking me in. I felt that the two of us were one as far as it was concerned. The expression on its porcine face was almost amusement. Although the wolf was more powerful, that wasn't going to stop the pig taking a bite. I and the wolf would have let these pig-things through to the new world, but gratitude wasn't part of their nature. Nor was respect for the hierarchy of the food chain. A wolf was more powerful than the pig, only to the point when the pig sank its teeth into the wolf's leg and didn't let go. The pig's giant body combined with its giant head meant it couldn't move fast, but it had few weak points. Once it had the sight and scent of food, there was little that would stop it. It would keep coming and coming. Sacrificing rest and sleep until it got to its prey. The only way to stop one was to throw a bigger meal into its path, but that wasn't an option. I and the wolf were the biggest meal on its horizon, and it was coming straight at us.

I could glimpse the land the pigs came from. Yellow and barren. Those pigs, and the bugs, and the crab as well, had stripped their own lands. It was time for them to make the journey to elsewhere. As I saw those worlds, I was conscious of this room – with the glowing writing on the walls and the rain and wind smashing against the windows – beginning to fade. One was being overlaid on top of the other. It was only a matter of time.

All these creatures, all this savagery we couldn't possibly understand or cope with, was going to pour through a tear in reality and flood our plane of existence. And the tear in reality was me. I was going to be the first one destroyed, and Ludo the first one consumed.

The Ravens Creature laughed and started to recite some words. A spell. It was trying to make all of this happen faster. Through desiccated lips, it spoke at the top of its voice, finding a high pitch almost like a kettle whistling. The words themselves were a gaggle of nonsense to me, but I knew what it was doing. I understood how close we were to the end.

My eyes went to Ludo, as he collapsed to the floor.

CHAPTER THIRTY-ONE

The Ravens Creature withdrew its finger and then turned its attention fully on me. Its eyes blazing, finding new depths of hellish fire. I saw it was everything it claimed to be. I could witness the truth in the recesses of its gaze. It had crossed dimensions, it had traversed other worlds, and it was going to bring them all to us,

Inside me, I could hear the tearing of claws and feel the wolf nearly at the surface. My face was ready to collapse. The lupine snout about to jut through, salivating and growling. Small consolation, but I was never going to see any of this terrible future I'd fleetingly envisaged. The flashes in my mind were brief previews, yet I wouldn't see this destruction unfold. I'd be torn apart long before then. Either the lycanthrope which took my place was going to escape into this terrifying new world, or it would be caught as one of the first victims, along with Ludo. Either way, I was going to be a blighted stain on a forgotten piece of ground in the land once called Wales. The place where the world ended.

I continued to scream within my mind and roar to the world, but beyond that, I was still paralysed. All my muscles were frozen to the spot, unable to do anything to prevent my fate. Completely hopeless in the face of the coming Armageddon.

"Excuse me," said Ludo.

If I'd been capable of flinching, I would have flinched. That could have been the moment to bring me out of it. But I was too rigid for any reaction. The Ravens Creature, for only the flicker of a second, did seem startled. It was almost impossible to read any emotions on its skeletal face, but I think it was surprised. However, it didn't turn its head in Ludo's direction.

"Just to clear things up," said Ludo, "you didn't make me fall. *I* made *me* fall. It felt I couldn't use my legs or my arms, which was an encumbrance. But I had a centre of gravity, and I found I could sort of lean it one way or another. And when I did, there were no feet to help me stumble a few steps, or no hands to grab onto anything. Which meant when I pushed myself backwards as hard as I could, there was nothing to stop me falling. But, since falling is movement, I realised as I made myself fall, that I was in control of my being and you were not." He grinned and bounced onto his feet. "What you're doing is all a trick, isn't it?"

He had posed the question and now waited for a reply, but The Ravens Creature simply continued to bore its eyes into mine, apparently ignoring Ludo.

But there was no way Ludo was going to be discounted.

"It's a mental trick," he went on. "You make us so petrified that we can't move. The fear centres in our minds are at such a pitch, it stops everything else. It obliterates all other emotions. You're desperate to maintain eye contact with Garris, aren't you? I stood stock still and Garris stood stock still. But I managed to fall backwards. I managed to regain control. So the question for Garris is, are you really howling or are you screaming?"

"*Yours* is the trick," said the Creature. "Things have gone too far for you to do anything to stop them."

I could only see Ludo from the corner of my eye, but he crossed his arms with utter confidence. He seemed completely unaffected by the peril we were in, by the possible end of the world.

"It seems to me," Ludo pressed on, "if Garris can do nothing more than howl, then that's bad. It's not good at all. It's not remotely a human sound, and shame on you for bringing my friend to this point. For putting him through such tortures. But, on the other hand, if with everything he is going through, he can force a human scream through his own lips, then that would be a good development. Or a yell. Or a laugh, I suppose – although I doubt Garris is in much of a mood for comedy. If he can make his own noise, rather than that of the beast allegedly inside him, then that's great. It means he's in there. It means, Mr Ravens Creature – or Mr Jacob Ravens, as you don't get to deny who you are so easily – that despite everything you're doing, we *do* have a chance."

And in the instant, I ceased howling. Ludo's words gave me the strength to do it. The howling stopped, my lips closed for merely an instant, and then I let loose an actual human scream. Only for a few seconds, but the voice from my lips and the voice inside my head matched.

I screamed.

Then, despite all I'd seen and everything I'd felt, I closed my mouth. After a cry coming ceaselessly from the depths of my lungs, I managed to quiet my terror. I was still panting, I remained fearful, I couldn't quite move yet, but I had the thinnest sliver of control.

"Excellent!" said Ludo, bouncing on his heels. "We can all talk without having to yell. Isn't that wonderful?"

"Do you believe you can stop me?" the Creature snarled.

"I don't know. But I'm going to try."

Rain smashed the windows – cracking the remaining panes – as if trying to prove to Ludo that his hopes were futile, but he ignored it.

Ludo moved across between The Ravens Creature and

me. "We've been told more than once that you're a trickster. And the thing with a trick is they only work if you can get the other person to buy into it. But we're past that particular point, aren't we? We're at the juncture where what you call magic no longer works. You don't have full control anymore. We're regaining it. So we've reached the moment where the best thing to do is try to talk things through." He gave a crooked smile. "You want to change the world, don't you?"

"You cannot say what I want. You cannot comprehend what I am. You are nothing compared to me."

"Oh, I don't know. I think you're fairly easy to read. You being you, you don't want to change it through your philanthropy. Instead, you want to smash everything apart. You're inviting who knows what through, to do who knows what. And when they carry out whatever destruction comes most naturally to them, you'll take a ringside seat. Does that sum things up?" Ludo shook his head. "The fact that you were dead gives you greater power, doesn't it? That's why you killed yourself in that New York hotel room, and why you made the arrangements for the alternative burial. You wanted more. You and your gang of loonies wanted to take apart the world which was beginning to stop appreciating you. Except you thought the resurrection would happen much sooner and that you'd look much better."

There were three visions before me. The world as it was, this strange room with its glowing writing and inclement weather outside, and latterly the back of Ludo Carstairs's head; then the worlds of the pig creatures and the giant bugs and the wolf (which seemed to be failing in its attempts to carve through me); and then there was the Creature's eyes, boring into me, piercing me, determined not to let me go.

"What is the circle by the way?" asked Ludo. "This room is a square."

"I am growing!" The Ravens Creature growled. "I am becoming the god I was meant to be, and I shall enjoy watching you being ripped apart."

It was said in a tone which didn't invite any further conversation, but The Ravens Creature didn't know Ludo well if it thought that was going to work.

"And all this is *growing* for you, is it?" said Ludo. "It's changing. As to be honest, I think it's you just being you, and not changing in the slightest. The thing with change – genuine change – is it's largely impossible unless you've reconciled yourself to your past. I'm not a psychotherapist, but that is my layman's interpretation. Unless you have accepted who you are and the things you have done, then how can you possibly change? If your understanding of yourself is a lie, or you are denying who you are, then you cannot change. You can only repeat the same patterns. And reaching into other dimensions to spit spite at the world feels exactly your pattern."

"You cannot claim to know me. The change is coming." Its eyes fixed on mine. Despite Ludo bobbing up and down before me and trying to block its baleful view.

There was a rumble of thunder above us.

Ludo continued: "I know what you're going to say, you are not a human. Or not fully human. As such, the normal rules do not apply to you. But the thing is, you grew from a human being. You might not want to admit it, you may see yourself as something *other,* but you are the twisted offshoot of the man who used to be Jacob Ravens. No! In fact, you *are* Jacob Ravens! It is his memories you are tapping into. It is his magic you are using. Maybe the other side of the world, a different version of him is trying to free himself from his coffin. But for now, all he has is you. A distillation of his soul, his mind and his spirit. You can't change those facts. You are not The Ravens Creature. You are not any other fancy or spooky name you care to call yourself. You *are* Jacob Ravens!"

The blow landed. "*I am beyond him!*"

"Maybe that's what you're telling yourself, but you are his essence, aren't you? I don't fully understand it myself, and look forward to putting our boffins on the case later so they can explain it all to me. But whatever was put into you was once a man named Jacob Ravens. You may not like the way you look in the mirror anymore, and you might have imagined yourself growing out of him over time, but you are at your core that same man."

The Ravens Creature finally moved its gaze from me, peering at Ludo and blazing all the more furiously.

"I am beyond all of you!" it repeated. "I am beyond this world!"

Ludo chuckled and jutted out his jaw.

"You say you want to change, but you are always going to be Jacob Ravens. There is no way around the fact. You may consider yourself something grand. And I agree, being able to burst open the doors of other universes puts you in a rare pantheon. But at your heart, you will never be anything other than a forgotten pulp novelist. That's all you are and all you ever will be."

"Prattle all you want," it sneered. "There's no halting the inevitable."

I swayed on my feet. The faintest hint of movement assailed my limbs.

"Or there is," said Ludo petulantly. "You are Jacob Ravens! And for all of your other worldly mysticism, he was a vain trickster of a man. True, as you are today, you might not be someone who is recognised by his parents, although your wife seems to have no problem falling into spousal behaviours. But you are Jacob Ravens, with all his strengths and limitations. He couldn't take control of those other worlds, so what on earth makes you imagine you can?"

The Ravens Creature emitted a low growl. Its fury building.

"Come on!" said Ludo. "You want me to stop talking, but I'm still talking. If you have this much control, why don't you make me stop?" He took a step closer to the creature. "There's something not right here, is there? I'm moving freely, why is that happening? Probably it's my fault for distracting you, I have received complaints that I talk too much. However, your plan was to use Garris to open these new vistas. But it doesn't look to me that Garris is a sturdy gate anymore, does he? In fact, I think you could knock him over with a feather."

Then Ludo turned and abruptly shoved, sending me sprawling across the room. I landed with a thud and a gasp of relief next to the polar bear's gaping mouth. Then seeing where I was, I scampered quickly to my left.

"Well, Ravens, are you not as strong as you want to be? Is your entire scheme reliant on parlour tricks which no longer work?" He chuckled. "Or is there a quality within you holding you back? Come on, Ravens, you've returned from the dead. Impressive. You're trying to reach into other worlds. Very impressive. But can you shut me up? That's the real challenge."

Ludo was so clear to me; but I could see those pigs coming nearer, along with the bugs and the crab with the one claw. The wolf continued to howl within my skull. There were other creatures as well. Red dragons and furry slugs and spiders with millions of rows of teeth. And men too. Giant Neanderthals with spears and clubs. They'd carved an existence in the brutal world of theirs, and would have no problem at all rising to the top of the food chain in ours. They had armies of the dead. Spirits which would raise corpses to join a battle. Similar to the one that had long-ago attached itself to poor Petula Glascock.

"Are you trying to upset me? You are such an insignificant man." The Ravens Creature at last managed to turn its anger into words. It fixed on me. Trying to summon me to my feet again.

"A little man who is below your contempt," said Ludo cheerfully. "The mere fact I'm talking suggests you're not as powerful as you think you are."

The elements kept hammering at the window. I watched two suns set in another world. I sensed a thousand different carnivores coming my way. Next to me, I heard an indistinct murmur of hunger from the polar bear, and scampered further across the floor. The Ravens Creature tried to pierce my mind, but I turned from its gaze.

Ludo began a slow circuit around The Ravens Creature.

"Do you want to hear why I've always avoided Jacob Ravens?" asked Ludo. "The reason I've not sullied myself with him is he always seemed to me the most appalling horror schlock. If I had encountered him as a teenage boy, I might have developed an unnatural interest in his scribblings. His stuff is written for teenage boys, isn't it? It has no higher aspiration than that. I've dipped in briefly, but a couple of short tales were enough for me." He smiled. "In this job, there is an unspoken recommendation that I read all of his work. *Your* work, I'm sorry, but I couldn't raise the interest to do so. What was the point after all?"

The Ravens Creature had no lips to pull back, but it was evident its teeth were bared.

"Come on!" goaded Ludo. He walked another circle around the creature. "Why don't you shut me up? Why don't you make Garris stand if he's going to be your gate? What's stopping you?"

I felt my own bones sag as The Ravens Creature fixed on him. I was soon to be gone from this world. My strength was fading. I was going to be ripped apart.

I clung onto the floor, desperate to keep hold of myself.

But the wolf growled louder in my mind.

"Of course, I may have misjudged his works," said Ludo. "All those theories the wide-eyed maniacs who call themselves fans espouse, that his work isn't fiction and is instead a roadmap to other universes. Tonight gives a kind of indication they were correct. Maybe those other universes are there and they are reachable. But, I'd still rather not read his books. As its turgid prose, isn't it? From what I've dipped into, Jacob Ravens – or yourself – cannot see a conjunction without adding to it and adding to it. Writing these horrible sprawling sentences which will inflict most readers with headaches." He sniffed. "Your wife doesn't appreciate your work either, does she?"

The elements howled harder, and the carcasses on the walls bawled and roared. The Ravens Creature's face seemed to burn.

My insides too were bubbling. I could move, but I still feared it was going to be over soon.

"Yes, I think I will remain a non-fan. Will you allow reading in this new world you're creating? I'm going to guess that books aren't going to have much of a future. After all, if you're spending a lot of time hunting for food and worrying about attacks from giant monsters, then you're not going to have a spare hour to curl up with an old yellowed Agatha Christie. And she is good. People want to actually enjoy escapism with her. But Jacob Ravens, not so much."

Ludo did another circle, very careful not to step near the growling mouths on the walls.

"And that would be a shame, wouldn't it? You're going to cause all this chaos, and those who survive will still forget about you. They'll have no notion you were behind it. You will be nothing, not even a footnote in future histories. It won't matter if – by some miracle – you can survive the oncoming storm in your crumbling body." He beamed, jutting his jaw in front of the creature. "You strived to be remembered when you were alive, didn't you, Jacob Ravens? Only no one remembers you. It took seventy years to get you out of the grave, despite the clues you left. And I suppose your legacy this time will be to create a new and terrifying world, but no one will remember you for it. In this awful new reality of yours, the name Jacob Ravens is going to have no more relevance than it has in our present world. There will not be a monument to your ego. Instead, when the first beast you encounter crunches on your bones, it will be testament to how much you have failed."

"*Enough!*"

The Ravens Creature lashed out and whacked Ludo on the side of the head. Its hands were more animal's claws than human fingers, and blood flew where the blow was struck.

Ludo collapsed to the floor, the wound spraying as he did.

Above us both, The Ravens Creature exhaled.

I scrabbled across the floor to check my friend was alive. Praying that the blow hadn't killed him.

"The circle has closed! The time has come!" The Ravens Creature bellowed, almost to himself. "The new world that is to come is mine!"

CHAPTER THIRTY-TWO

Ludo had a pulse, but the amount of blood coming from his head worried me. He wasn't going to have a pulse for much longer if he kept bleeding so profusely. His jaw moved, but the only sound was the faintest murmur. I doubted there was much sense in it.

I stared at The Ravens Creature. It was floating. Anger crackling off it. Whatever was transpiring, Ludo's insults hadn't done anything to stop it. The awful thought occurred that they might even have accelerated it.

The storm continued to rage, but it was as if it was one step removed from us. It wasn't quite outside anymore; not truly in our reality. The words on the walls appeared likely to explode into an apocalyptic flame in an instant.

A foot or so off the ground, lightning crackled around the creature's face. The fury which had been provoked by Ludo metamorphosed into mad glee. Toothless as it was, a rictus smile rose into its desiccated features.

"It is happening!" it called. "It is coming through to us!"

The image of the wolf flashed into my mind. Its mouth wide. Strong again. Pouncing in on me, ready to devour me whole.

I blinked away as much of the vision as I could. Trying

to focus only on this world, and not what was coming. Shaking, I attempted to rouse Ludo.

The wind howled around the building.

"The circle will hold and a new world will be born!" croaked the creature. "My world."

I reached my arm around Ludo and readied myself to hoist him up. I could move and my mouth now opened to speak, but I had no idea whether I could find my voice. When it came, it was with a croak of exertion.

"Ravens, I've seen the other side!" I whispered. "Are you seriously going to let all those things through here? Have you seen those creatures? What they can do? If you let them loose, *everything* will be gone."

Apparently aware they were being talked about, the entities from beyond asserted themselves. Filling my mind's vision. The crab beast with the one eye and the one claw sank its incisor into me and twisted it around. My spine arched on the floor and I screamed from my depths.

My terror plucked Ludo somewhat from his daze. He sat up unsteadily, blinking. His hands went to his eyes, and he tried to wipe the blood from them.

The other worlds were before me. More real than anything in this abandoned dwelling in Wales. The only men who survived in the realms beyond were the fiercest and most gore-soaked. Bolstered by their armies of the dead. There were millions of them and they were larger and stronger than the homo sapiens of our world. Even with our advanced weaponry, we were going to find it impossible to defeat such armies.

I managed to stop screaming and gasped. Rolling to my left I vomited through fear and pain. The cheese and laverbread making a reappearance as a thin goo.

Ludo continued trying to wipe the blood from his eyes. His disorientation wasn't hard to notice, as his fingers missed their target and ran across his cheeks.

I glanced at the words on the walls: so bright red, smoke was billowing off them. They were burning away the brick they were carved into. In a few moments, this building was going to be blown apart by whatever came through me. The stench of burning tickled my nostrils and nearly made me sick again. Those symbols were all the way around the room and the door was locked behind us. There was no way I could open it. We were trapped.

This room, with its runes, was the circle.

It had been created for this very purpose. Even before Jacob Ravens's rise to prominence. Professor Thorpe had built it with this terrible future in mind. Then the real Ravens had seen these worlds. He'd written about them and then, after his death, his acolytes in their nihilism wanted to bring them into ours.

The wind and rain continued to hammer the window, but everything else about our own world seemed farther and farther away.

I tried to stand, but felt like an old man who needed sticks to make it anywhere. My feet slipped beneath me. It wasn't made easier by me simultaneously trying to pull Ludo to his feet, bringing us up together. Finally, somehow, we stood in front of The Ravens Creature. Facing the reanimated Jacob Ravens. Ludo half-hanging from under my right arm, but at least he was with it enough to put his own arm around my waist.

The Creature's eyes burned towards me, but not quite with the same intensity as before. Or maybe it was because all the words in this room were burning with exactly the same ferocity.

It had wanted to hold me in place, to make sure I didn't do anything to interfere with its plans, but I *could* move.

I jutted my own jaw forward, trying to show as much defiance as Ludo had evinced. "You say the circle is complete," I said. "But is it really?"

And then I ran. Dragging Ludo with me and finding with relief that his legs worked too. I had to half carry him, but he tried his best. I hunched, so my head and shoulders were bowed.

At first The Ravens Creature glared at us, unable to understand this further defiance. But then came the shriek, the gasp of horror as it must have realised what I intended.

The room was secure. Those walls around us were solid and the heavy door was firmly shut. If I got too near the walls, I might burn myself to death before anything else happened. That's if one of the animal heads didn't take a bite from me first. But there was one weak point. Even if it seemed distant to me.

Ludo under my arm, I charged at the window. And when I was two feet from it, the words glowing below the sill ahead of me, I leapt head-first with Ludo clamped tight to my side and crashed through the window frame.

Behind us, The Ravens Creature wailed.

CHAPTER THIRTY-THREE

It could have been the window was no longer in our world, that it was an illusion, and to jump at it was to jump into a void. Or it could have been that it remained an actual presence, but was much more solid than I could possibly have guessed, in which case Ludo and I were liable to bounce off it and land broken on the floor. It could have been we were utterly trapped.

But no, the wood splintered and the remaining glass shattered. Then we were outside, plummeting through the cold, wet Welsh air. I landed with a thud. Ludo had slipped from my grasp, but I heard him groan as he hit the ground somewhere nearby.

I glanced at the room we'd exited. It was burning. The words having finally caught aflame. Such was the heat, the rest of the building was catching too. Then I saw the face of The Ravens Creature. It was glaring after us.

Ludo had landed a little ahead of me, and his face had splattered into the mud. The idea came to me in a second. I grabbed a lump of soil and smeared it to the cut on his forehead. He would have to have it cleaned properly later, and I guessed there was a chance of blood poisoning, but it clogged the wound. If we had to worry about getting treatment for septicaemia later, then at least we'd have survived. At least there would still be things like doctors and hospitals.

His eyes didn't possess the full Ludo Carstairs spark, but I could see he was beginning to focus. He might be dazed, but he was recovering his senses.

"Come on, Ludo!" I yelled, trying to be heard over the storm and The Ravens Creature's screams behind us. "The circle has broken. That room had magic sewn through its walls. It was in the words. But we're not in there, we made it out. But we have to get away from it, Ludo! We have to *run*!"

My shouts took a moment, but they managed to get through. He was groggy and uncoordinated, but he forced himself to his feet.

Behind us, The Ravens Creature yelled. Words and phrases from long-dead languages. There were a few seconds of pain, as I felt the wolf's incisors slip into me, but I pushed myself on. I had to keep moving. Wrapped around each other, we ran. Trying to keep upright, and not to trip in any of the divots in the soil. Doing our utmost to get away from The Ravens Creature before the world ended.

CHAPTER THIRTY-FOUR

"Don't look back!" Ludo cried. His voice thick. "Don't let yourself look at it."

I sensed he was right. The story of Lot's wife came to me. Fleeing Sodom and Gomorrah, and ignoring the command not to peer at it. We were free of the circle, we had broken clear of those mystic words, but so much magic remained within the air. I didn't know how far it stretched, or how much even lingered within me. I had no idea whether we had done enough to prevent a sundering.

Behind us came the cries of thwarted fury, accompanied by a crackling. It was like something being torn apart. An entity broken and destroyed. The fear came that we'd failed, and it was the sound of our world ending. Of a new reality bursting through.

Part of me wanted to turn around and stare at it, to see what was happening. But I knew if I did, I might be caught. That the sight of it – and the sight of whatever The Ravens Creature had conjured in its desperation – would not let me go. I needed to be far away. I must not gaze upon it.

The two of us ran. Ludo holding me upright, as much as I was supporting him.

I could hear what could only be described as a collapse.

Not just walls of bricks and mortar falling in on themselves, but something much deeper and more comprehensive. The Ravens Creature had summoned a new reality, and it had nowhere to go.

Ludo's voice was breathless, but clearly his mind was working faster. "You disrupted the spell, but it's got a hell of a lot of power. Something bad is going to happen if we're near. We have to get away, Garris. We definitely have to get *you* from there. The magic had you staring at The Ravens Creature. Make sure you continue to look away!"

He was right. It sounded like a whirlpool behind me. I could feel the clutching of a zephyr at my back, and knew if I turned my head, I'd be sucked into its vortex. That's all it would take. One curious glance. A look at what was happening, and I'd be sliding towards it. I'd be the gate once more.

Beside me, Ludo tripped on a grassy clump and lost his footing. He stumbled forward. I just about held him. Pulling him along, as at the same time he hauled me along. There was a weariness to my step. The whirlpool was behind me and it was tugging at me, but I couldn't stop. I couldn't fall. I had to keep going or it would be the end of everything.

Amidst the noise, I heard screaming. I hoped it was The Ravens Creature. That it was crying at the destruction of its dreams. But the dread notion came to me that it wasn't The Ravens Creature in anger, but exulting in triumph. I had the horrible impression that the noise was of something else coming through to our world. Not the wolf. As I could still feel it trapped inside me, howling that its freedom had been thwarted. But others had come close enough, they might have found another tear in realities. Those greased pig-things with the straw-coloured hair, or the crab, or one of those huge Neanderthals. Perhaps, despite our efforts, we had failed. The end of our reality was looming. But the only way to confirm any of those dreads was to stop and look back. And I couldn't do that. I had to avert my gaze and keep running.

We were nearly at the edge of the basin. The slope up was directly ahead. I didn't know if I could do it. Ludo had mud smeared all over his face to stop the bleeding, and I couldn't be sure if he could do it either. Whatever was happening behind was akin to an H-bomb, I imagined. We couldn't look back, but we couldn't get away. Neither of us had slept properly in days, and the weariness was finally going to overwhelm us. Human frailty would be our downfall.

We each dashed at the sides of the basin. Our legs slipping beneath us, we were soon on all fours, hands clinging on to the grass for any purchase we could get. The weather had been so horrific, that even if we'd had a lot of time to get to the top of the slope, it would have been near impossible to do so without slipping in the mud. It was inevitable we'd slide down towards the base, and thus be trapped near the grim ruin and our certain doom. There was no way we were going to escape. We were going to fail here. Everything was going to end.

And then behind us was a loud *pop*. It wasn't the big bang of the end of the world I'd been dreading. Instead it was a dull distant sound of a bubble disappearing. In response, the calamitous noise eased. Even the weather seemed to calm in an instant.

I found myself lying face-down in the mud, not knowing what to do. Scared of turning around to check what had happened, but knowing I had to, eventually. That lethal curiosity urge.

It was Ludo who turned first, his face half-covered in dirt, a grimy Phantom of the Opera. He stared towards the ruined building with narrow and fearful eyes, and then he tapped my arm and gave a thumb up to indicate it was okay for me to look as well.

I peered slowly, expecting to see the building in bits. But there was nothing. A crater where the dwelling had been. Blackened soil in a circle, as if dynamite had been used. There were no horrific wild creatures, no strange lands from beyond crashing into our world. And no Ravens Creature.

Jacob Ravens wasn't there.

"It opened a gap," said Ludo, breathless. "But then it fell into it. Much like falling into a black hole, I guess."

We had broken the circle, I had removed myself from its gaze and I had thwarted the spell. Every inch of me ached, but – for today, at least – we had won.

Together Ludo and I stared at it, mouths slightly agape. It being Wales, after all, the rain started to get heavier.

CHAPTER THIRTY-FIVE

"You don't think it's completely over, do you?" I asked.

We had waited on the dock and, as good as her word, we could see in the distance Angharad steering her boat towards us.

Ludo sat on the edge of the old wooden dock, his feet hanging above the water. Despite his bloody and muddy face, and his stained and ruined suit and raincoat, he could almost have been an urchin on his summer holiday.

"For today, yes. I think we've done what we needed to do. I don't think that's the end of the Jacob Ravens saga though."

"Why not?"

He turned and regarded me with a smile. "Come on, Garris. Do you truly believe this is over? I know you're an optimist by nature, but there are good feelings and then there are facts."

"No," I agreed. "I don't think it's done."

His attention reverted to the waves. "Do you still have the wolf inside you?"

"I don't know."

"Yes you do know. Do you?"

I nodded.

"Just as I thought. There is a creature within you from another world. It will no doubt fancy its chances of eventually opening the doors between these worlds and climbing out. Then there's the question of what happened to The Ravens Creature?"

"It's like you said to him about the toppling," I said. "It seems to me that when he couldn't open the gate properly, he and the building got sucked through in the other direction. Whether that means the hole has been plugged, I cannot say. I hope it's the case, but we'll have to send a more expert team in."

Angharad's boat moved in closer. The sea was calmer this morning.

"It's not a bad hypothesis," he mused. "My view isn't too far from it. But I doubt something so simple would completely stop The Ravens Creature. When he was a man named Jacob Ravens, he was able to traverse between other dimensions. As such, I doubt such a thing as arriving in the wrong place is going to be fatal for him."

"So you think the creature will be back?"

He pondered for half a minute, kicking his feet forward as if they could touch the waves below. "Don't get me wrong, Garris," he said. "We have done a good job today. We have done a good job the last couple of days. Everything could have ended last night, and you stopped it."

"*We* stopped it."

"Don't be so modest. I was a passenger at the end. The thing is, however, it's a creature which has already found a way to return from the dead once, and that was after it blew its own brains out. I doubt anything like dimensional displacement – if that's the term I'm looking for – would halt it. Such a thing would end you and me forever, but not The Ravens Creature."

"As I said, I'll get a full team on it. See what we can find."

"It almost certainly won't be much," he said. "But let's not be pessimistic. Let's enjoy ourselves for now. As our beloved Chief has said more than once, you never know what threat tomorrow might bring."

He jumped up onto his feet. The dock rattled a little, but he wasn't fazed.

"We need to celebrate, Garris. There was something here tonight which could have destroyed the world, and we stopped it succeeding, which is a good day's work in my eyes. I think we owe ourselves a slap-up breakfast."

"I'd like a shower first."

Our yellow raincoats were nearly as brown and dirty as our suits underneath.

He chuckled. "Good call! Maybe we could buy some new suits along the way. I'm proud of you, by the way, Garris."

"What do you mean? It was you who broke the spell. It was you who proved what a trickster he was. It was you with the jabs at his vanity."

He looked towards the approaching Angharad.

"But it was you who actually broke the circle. Even after everything which happened, you didn't quit. You kept going, hunting for a way out. You didn't let the wolf take you."

"It was a team effort."

He nodded. "I'll take that. You know, I think I owe The Sons an apology."

"What?" There was half surprise and half a chuckle in my tone.

"Yes. They were of course thinking of their profit margin, but I think they were also trying to think of the greater good when they attempted to persuade us not to come here."

"The greater good?"

"I know." He laughed. "Who would have thought they could behave in such a fashion? Earl Henderson gave us the information he had, but it was really Emilia Ravens who was the duplicitous lure in the trap. Doing what her one-time husband wanted, while giving every indication she hated him."

I waved at Angharad, but she didn't wave back.

"Emilia Ravens has also disappeared."

"Quite. They're well matched. And much like her husband, we can try to find her another day."

"Another day is correct." I sighed. "For now, I simply want to get off this rock."

"I agree," he said, standing at my shoulder in anticipation. "Let's get a change of clothes, a shower and a nap. Then maybe we can have dinner in London tonight. Beryl too."

"She'll be delighted to see you, Ludo."

The boat came into the dock and Angharad watched us wanly at us over the wheel. Seemingly not surprised by how crumpled and muddy we had now become.

Again I waved at her, and again she didn't wave back.

Irrationally, I had a vague sense of trouble. But surely it couldn't mean anything.

Meeting her eye I smiled, and she gave the thinnest smile in return.

I swallowed. It was times like this that I was grateful not to be clairvoyant.

AUTHOR'S NOTE

I hope you've enjoyed the fifth Ludo Carstairs novel.

The way I've been thinking of this series is as a ten part television season. Standalone adventures, but building things up to a grand conclusion. Since the first five have come out so close together, this is a sort of a mid-season break. Ludo Carstairs and Michael Garris finally encountering the big bad guy who was first mentioned to them in THE NEMESIS TOUCH.

If you've read my author notes for the previous Ludo Carstairs novels, then you know I'm leaning into a mythology I established in my Ghostly Shadows series. Far be it from me to set any homework, but if you are interested in finding out more, then Jacob Ravens appears in THE HELLBOUND DETECTIVE, along with his wife. Emilia Ravens also appears (kind of) in TERROR OF BREAKSPEAR HALL.

While Elspeth Carmine not only appears in THE NEMESIS TOUCH, but also in THE CALLER.

If you enjoyed what you read in this volume, I'd be most grateful if you could say as much in a review on Amazon. I don't have a large marketing team behind me. In fact, I am doing all this by myself; as such, reviews are my lifeblood. So, if you could take five minutes of your day to post one, I'd be thrilled.

Thank you for reading THE UNDEAD RAVENS. I hope to see you return next year for THE WRAITH ASSASSIN.

Happy reading, all!

FRJ.

Get ready for the next Ludo Carstairs Supernatural Thriller!

THE WRAITH ASSASSIN

Will Ludo survive the ultimate killer?

Ludo Carstairs and Michael Garris are taking an important package to their HQ in London. A defector. An enemy agent who has promised to tell them a thousand secrets.

But they are waylaid. A white-faced creature made of shadows burst from the sky and tears apart the train carriage in which they're travelling. It snatches the defector from their grasp, but not before it's twisted and shifted its face so the features perfectly mimic Ludo's.

A day later, they meet with a researcher who has become obsessed with something she calls *The Wraith*. A netherworld creature who now works as a paid killer. One which can change its face, defy gravity and disappear into the darkness. In her strange old house, she has a huge amount of information about this myth, but Ludo realises The Wraith itself is also in residence.

In a heartbeat, Ludo has gone. Kidnapped. Vanished.

Garris is desperate to get him back. From Venice, to a strange abandoned monastery on the African coast, he sets out on the trail of his partner…

Can he get to him in time, or will The Wraith do its worst?

ABOUT F.R. JAMESON

F.R. Jameson was born in Wales, but now lives with his wife and daughter in London. He writes both horror and thrillers. The thrillers are sometimes of the supernatural variety, and sometimes historical, set around the British film industry.

You can find him on Facebook, and follow him on Twitter, Instagram and Pinterest: @frjameson.

Printed in Great Britain
by Amazon